TRUE NAMES

"The story is a marvelous mixture of hard-science SF and sword-and-sorcery imagery. Vinge posits that in a direct neurocybernetic interface, the information would be analogized by the brain into symbols it is comfortable with. The "place" in which the Coven "meets," for example, is or seems to be a castle, guarded by a program which manifests itself as a firebreathing dragon, sitting in a magma moat, wearing an asbestos T-shirt. Fail to satisfy it, and it will "kill" you, dumping you back into the real world—a fate most Wizards seem to regard as very little better than death.

"Vinge set himself about fifteen challenges in this story, any one of which might have wrecked a lesser writer, and pulled them all off with appalling ease. No point in listing them all—but the most important one to my mind is this: he succeeded in making me *feel,* for over an hour, what it is like to be more than human. That is one of SF's major challenges, and it is bloody hard to do.

"Do not miss this ingenious and truly original story—it is one of those that, when you're done, you wish the author were present so you could applaud."
—*Analog* Magazine

Other books by Vernor Vinge:

GRIMM'S WORLD

THE WITLING

THE PEACE WAR (available from Bluejay Books)

TRUE NAMES

VERNOR VINGE

Bluejay Books Inc.

All the characters in this book are fictitious, and any resemblance to actual persons, living or dead, is coincidental.

A Bluejay Book, published by arrangement with the Author.

For information, contact Bluejay Books Inc., 130 West Forty-second Street, New York, New York 10036.

Manufactured in the United States of America

First Bluejay printing: November 1984

To my sister,
  Patricia Vinge,
with Love.

In the once upon a time days of the First Age of Magic, the prudent sorcerer regarded his own true name as his most valued possession but also the greatest threat to his continued good health, for—the stories go—once an enemy, even a weak unskilled enemy, learned the sorcerer's true name, then routine and widely known spells could destroy or enslave even the most powerful. As times passed, and we graduated to the Age of Reason and thence to the first and second industrial revolutions, such notions were discredited. Now it seems that the Wheel has turned full circle (even if there never really was a First Age) and we are back to worrying about true names again:

The first hint Mr. Slippery had that his own True Name might be known—and, for that matter, known to the Great Enemy—came with the appearance of two black Lincolns humming up the long dirt driveway that stretched through the dripping pine forest down

to Road 29. Roger Pollack was in his garden weeding, had been there nearly the whole morning, enjoying the barely perceptible drizzle and the overcast, and trying to find the initiative to go inside and do work that actually makes money. He looked up the moment the intruders turned, wheels squealing, into his driveway. Thirty seconds passed, and the cars came out of the third-generation forest to pull up beside and behind Pollack's Honda. Four heavy-set men and a hard-looking female piled out, started purposefully across his well-tended cabbage patch, crushing tender young plants with a disregard which told Roger that this was no social call.

Pollack looked wildly around, considered making a break for the woods, but the others had spread out and he was grabbed and frog-marched back to his house. (Fortunately the door had been left unlocked. Roger had the feeling that they might have knocked it down rather than ask him for the key.) He was shoved abruptly into a chair. Two of the heaviest and least collegiate-looking of his visitors stood on either side of him. Pollack's protests—now just being voiced—brought no response. The woman and an older man poked around among his sets. "Hey, I remember this, Al: It's the script for *1965*. See?" The woman spoke as she flipped through the holo-scenes that decorated the interior wall.

The older man nodded. "I told you. He's written more popular games than any three men and even more than some agencies. Roger Pollack is something of a genius."

They're novels, damn you, not games! Old irritation flashed unbidden into Roger's mind. Aloud: "Yeah, but most of my fans aren't as persistent as you all."

"Most of your fans don't know that you are a criminal, Mr. Pollack."

"Criminal? I'm no criminal—but I do know my rights. You FBI types must identify yourselves, give me a phone call, and—"

The woman smiled for the first time. It was not a nice smile. She was about thirty-five, hatchet-faced, her hair drawn back in the single braid favored by military types. Even so it could have been a nicer smile. Pollack felt a chill start up his spine. "Perhaps that would be true, if we *were* the FBI or if you were *not* the scum you are. But this is a Welfare Department bust, Pollack, and you are suspected—putting it kindly—of interference with the instrumentalities of National and individual survival."

She sounded like something out of one of those asinine scripts he occasionally had to work on for government contracts. Only now there was nothing to laugh about, and the cold between his shoulder-blades spread. Outside the drizzle had become a misty rain sweeping across the Northern California forests. Normally he found that rain a comfort, but now it just added to the gloom. Still, if there was any chance he could wriggle out of this, it would be worth the effort. "Okay, so you have license to hassle innocents, but sooner or later you're going to discover that I *am* innocent and then you'll find out what hostile media coverage can really be like." *And thank God I backed up my files last night. With luck, all they'll find is some out-of-date stock-market schemes.*

"You're no innocent, Pollack. An *honest* citizen is content with an ordinary data set like yours there."

She pointed across the living room at the forty-by-fifty-centimeter data set. It was the great-grandchild of the old CRTs. With color and twenty-line-per-millimeter resolution, it was the standard of government offices and the more conservative industries. There was a visible layer of dust on Pollack's model. The femcop moved quickly across the living room and poked into the drawers under the picture window. Her maroon business suit revealed a thin and angular figure. "An *honest* citizen would settle for a standard processor and a few thousand megabytes of fast storage." With some superior intuition she pulled open the center drawer—right under the marijuana plants—to reveal at least five hundred cubic centimeters of optical memory, neatly racked and threaded through to the next drawer which held correspondingly powerful CPUs. Even so, it was nothing compared to the gear he had buried under the house.

She drifted out into the kitchen and was back in a moment. The house was a typical airdropped bungalow, small and easy to search. Pollack had spent most of his money on the land and his . . . hobbies. "And finally," she said, a note of triumph in her voice, "an *honest* citizen does not need one of these!" She had finally spotted the Other World gate. She waved the electrodes in Pollack's face.

"Look, in spite of what you may want, all this is still legal. In fact, that gadget is scarcely more powerful than an ordinary games interface." That should be a good explanation, considering that he was a novelist.

The older man spoke almost apologetically, "I'm afraid Virginia has a tendency to play cat and mouse,

Mr. Pollack. You see, we know that in the Other World you are Mr. Slippery."

"Oh."

There was a long silence. Even "Virginia" kept her mouth shut. This had been, of course, Roger Pollack's great fear. They had discovered Mr. Slippery's True Name and it was Roger Andrew Pollack TIN/SSAN 0959-34-2861, and no amount of evasion, tricky programming, or robot sources could ever again protect him from them. "How did you find out?"

A third cop, a technician type, spoke up. "It wasn't easy. We wanted to get our hands on someone who was really good, not a trivial vandal—what your Coven would call a lesser warlock." The younger man seemed to know the jargon, but you could pick that up just by watching the daily paper. "For the last three months, DoW has been trying to find the identity of someone of the caliber of yourself or Robin Hood, or Erythrina, or the Slimey Limey. We were having no luck at all until we turned the problem around and began watching artists and novelists. We figured at least a fraction of them must be attracted to vandal activities. And they would have the talent to be good at it. Your participation novels are the best in the world." There was genuine admiration in his voice. *One meets fans in the oddest places,* "so you were one of the first people we looked at. Once we suspected you, it was just a matter of time before we had the evidence."

It was what he had always worried about. A successful warlock cannot afford to be successful in the real world. He had been greedy; he loved both realms too much.

The older cop continued the technician's almost diffident approach. "In any case, Mr. Pollack, I think you realize that if the Federal government wants to concentrate all its resources on the apprehension of a single vandal, we can do it. The vandals' power comes from their numbers rather than their power as individuals."

Pollack repressed a smile. That was a common belief—or faith—within government. He had snooped on enough secret memos to realize that the Feds really believed it, but it was very far from true. He was not nearly as clever as someone like Erythrina. He could only devote fifteen or twenty hours a week to SIG activities. Some of the others must be on welfare, so complete was their presence on the Other Plane. The cops had nailed him simply because he was a relatively easy catch.

"So you have something besides jail planned for me?"

"Mr. Pollack, have you ever heard of the Mailman?"

"You mean on the Other Plane?"

"Certainly. He has had no notoriety in the, uh, real world as yet."

For the moment there was no use lying. They must know that no member of a SIG or coven would ever give his True Name to another member. There was no way he could betray any of the others—*he hoped.*

"Yeah, he's the weirdest of the werebots."

"Werebots?"

"Were-robots, like werewolves—get it? They don't really mesh with coven imagery. They want some new mythos, and this notion that they are humans who can turn into machines seems to suit them. It's too dry for me. This Mailman, for instance, never uses real time communication. If you want anything from him, you usually have to wait a day or two for each response—just like the old-time hardcopy mail service."

"That's the fellow. How impressed are you by him?"

"Oh, we've been aware of him for a couple years, but he's so slow that for a long time we thought he was some clown on a simple data set. Lately, though, he's pulled some really—" Pollack stopped short, remembering just who he was gossiping with.

"—some really tuppin stunts, eh, Pollack?" The femcop "Virginia" was back in the conversation. She pulled up one of the roller chairs, till her knees were almost touching his, and stabbed a finger at his chest. "You may not know just how tuppin. You vandals have caused Social Security Records enormous problems, and Robin Hood cut IRS revenues by three percent last year. You and your friends are a greater threat than any foreign enemy. Yet you're nothing compared to this Mailman."

Pollack was rocked back. It must be that he had seen only a small fraction of the Mailman's japes. "You're actually scared of him," he said mildly.

Virginia's face began to take on the color of her suit. Before she could reply, the older cop spoke. "Yes, we are scared. We can scarcely cope with the Robin Hoods and the Mr. Slipperys of the world. Fortunately, most vandals are interested in personal gain or in proving their cleverness. They realize that if they cause too much trouble, they could no doubt be identified. I suspect that tens of thousands of cases of Welfare and Tax fraud are undetected, committed by little people with simple equipment who succeed because they don't steal much—perhaps just their own income tax liability—and don't wish the notoriety which you, uh, warlocks go after. If it weren't for their petty individualism, they would be a greater threat than the nuclear terrorists.

"But the Mailman is different: he appears to be ideologically motivated. He is *very* knowledgeable, *very* powerful. Vandalism is not enough for him; he wants control . . ." The Feds had no idea how long it had been going on, at least a year. It never would have been discovered but for a few departments in the Federal Screw Standards Commission which kept their principal copy records on paper. Discrepancies showed up between those records and the decisions rendered in the name of the FSSC. Inquiries were made; computer records were found at variance with the hardcopy. More inquiries. By luck more than anything else, the investigators discovered that decision modules as well as data were different from the hardcopy backups. For thirty years government had depended on automated central planning, shifting more and more from legal descriptions of decision algorithms to program representations that could work directly with data bases to allocate resources, suggest legislation, outline military strategy.

The take-over had been subtle, and its extent was unknown. That was the horror of it. It was not even clear just what groups within the Nation (or without) were benefitting from the changed interpretations of Federal law and resource allocation. Only the decision modules in the older departments could be directly checked, and some thirty percent of them showed tampering. ". . .and that percentage scares us as much as anything, Mr. Pollack. It would take a large team of technicians and lawyers *months* to successfully make just the changes that we have detected."

"What about the military?" Pollack thought of the Finger of God installations and the thousands of missiles pointed at virtually every country on Earth. If Mr. Slippery had ever desired to take over the world, that is what he would have gone for. To hell with pussy-footing around with Social Security checks.

"No. No penetration there. In fact, it was his attempt to infiltrate—" the older cop glanced hesitantly at Virginia, and Pollack realized who was the boss of this operation, "—NSA that revealed the culprit to be the Mailman. Before that it was anonymous, totally without the ego-flaunting we see in big-time vandals. But the military and NSA have their own systems. Impractical though that is, it paid off this time." Pollack nodded. The SIG steered clear of the military, and especially of NSA.

"But if he was able to slide through DoW and Department of Justice defenses so easy, you really don't know how much a matter of luck it was that he didn't also succeed with his first try on NSA. . . . I think I understand now. You need help. You hope to get some member of the Coven to work on this from the inside."

"It's not a *hope*, Pollack," said Virginia. "It's a certainty. Forget about going to jail. Oh, we could put you away forever on the basis of some of Mr. Slippery's pranks. But even if we don't do that, we can take away your license to operate. You know what that means."

It was not a question, but Pollack knew the answer nevertheless: ninety-eight percent of the jobs in modern society involved some use of a data set. Without a license, he was virtually unemployable—and that left Welfare, the prospect of sitting in some urbapt counting flowers on the wall. Virginia must have seen the defeat in his eyes. "Frankly, I am not as confident as Ray that you are all that sharp. But you are the best we could catch. NSA thinks we have a chance of finding the Mailman's true identity if we can get an agent into your coven. We want you to continue to attend coven meetings, but now your chief goal is not mischief but the gathering of information about the Mailman. You are to recruit any help you can without revealing that you are working for the government—you might even make up the story that you suspect the Mailman of being a government plot. (I'm sure you see he has some of the characteristics of a Federal agent working off a conventional data set.) Above all, you are to remain alert to contact from us, and give us your instant cooperation in anything we require of you. Is all this perfectly clear, Mr. Pollack?"

He found it difficult to meet her gaze. He had never really been exposed to extortion before. There was something . . . dehumanizing about being used so. "Yeah," he finally said.

"Good." She stood up, and so did the others. "If you behave, this is the last time you'll see us in person."

Pollack stood too. "And afterward, if you're . . . satisfied with my performance?"

Virginia grinned, and he knew he wasn't going to

Vernor Vinge

like her answer. "Afterward, we can come back to considering *your* crimes. If you do a good job, I would have no objection to your retaining a standard data set, maybe some of your interactive graphics. But I'll tell you, if it weren't for the Mailman, nabbing Mr. Slippery would make my month. There is no way I'd risk your continuing to abuse the System."

Three minutes later, their sinister black Lincolns were halfway down the drive, disappearing into the pines. Pollack stood in the drizzle watching till long after their sound had faded to nothing. He was barely aware of the cold wet across his shoulders and down his back. He looked up suddenly, feeling the rain in his face, wondering if the Feds were so clever that they had taken the day into account: the military's recon satellites could no doubt monitor their cars, but the civilian satellites the SIG had access to could not penetrate these clouds. Even if some other member of the SIG did know Mr. Slippery's True Name, they would not know that the Feds had paid him a visit.

Pollack looked across the yard at his garden. *What a difference an hour can make.*

By late afternoon, the overcast was gone. Sunlight glinted off millions of waterdrop jewels in the trees. Pollack waited till the sun was behind the tree line, till all that was left of its passage was a gold band across the taller trees to the east of his bungalow. Then he sat down before his equipment and prepared to ascend to the Other Plane. What he was undertaking was trickier than anything he had tried before, and he wanted to take as much time as the Feds would tolerate. A week of thought and research would have suited him more, but Virginia and her pals were clearly too impatient for that.

He powered up his processors, settled back in his favorite chair, and carefully attached the Portal's five sucker electrodes to his scalp. For long minutes nothing happened: a certain amount of self-denial—or at least self-hypnosis—was necessary to make the ascent. Some experts recommended drugs or sensory isolation to heighten the user's sensitivity to the faint, ambiguous signals that could be read from the Portal. Pollack, who was certainly more experienced than any of the pop experts, had found that he could make it simply by staring out into the trees and listening to the wind-surf that swept through their upper branches.

And just as a daydreamer forgets his actual surroundings and sees other realities, so Pollack drifted, detached, his subconscious interpreting the status of the West Coast communication and data services as a vague thicket for his conscious mind to inspect, interrogate for the safest path to an intermediate haven. Like most exurb data-commuters, Pollack rented the standard optical links: Bell, Boeing, Nippon Electric. Those, together with the local West Coast data companies, gave him more than enough paths to proceed with little chance of detection to any accepting processor on Earth. In minutes, he had traced through three changes of carrier and found a place to do his intermediate computing. The comsats rented processor time almost as cheaply as ground stations, and an automatic payment transaction (through several dummy accounts set up over the last several years) gave him sole control of a large data space within milliseconds of his request. The whole process was almost at a subconscious level—the proper functioning of numerous routines he and others had devised over the last four years. Mr. Slippery (the other name was avoided now, even in his thoughts) had achieved the fringes of the Other Plane. He took a quick peek through the eyes of a low-resolution weather satellite, saw the North American continent spread out below, the terminator sweeping through the West, most of the plains clouded over. One never knew when some apparently irrelevant information might help—and though it could all be done automatically through subconscious access, Mr. Slippery had always been a romantic about spaceflight.

He rested for a few moments, checking that his indirect communication links were working and that the encryption routines appeared healthy, untampered with. (Like most folks, honest citizens or warlocks, he had no trust for the government standard encryption routines, but preferred the schemes that had leaked out of academia—over NSA's petulant objections—during the last fifteen years.) Protected now against traceback, Mr. Slippery set out for the Coven itself. He quickly picked up the trail, but this was never an easy trip, for the SIG members had no interest in being bothered by the unskilled.

In particular, the traveler must be able to take advantage of subtle sensory indications, and see in them the environment originally imagined by the SIG. The correct path had the aspect of a narrow row of stones cutting through a gray-greenish swamp. The air was cold but very moist. Weird, towering plants dripped audibly onto the faintly iridescent water and the broad lilies. The subconscious knew what the stones represented, handled the chaining of routines from one information net to another, but it was the conscious mind of the skilled traveler that must make the decisions that could lead to the gates of the Coven, or to the symbolic "death" of a dump back to the real world. The basic game was a distant relative of the ancient Adventure that had been played on computer systems for more than forty years, and a nearer relative of the participation novels that are still widely sold. There were two great differences, though. This game was more serious, and was played at a level of complexity impossible without the use of the EEG input/output that the warlocks and the popular data bases called Portals.

There was much misinformation and misunderstanding about the Portals. Oh, responsible data bases like the *LA Times* and the *CBS News* made it clear that there was nothing supernatural about them or about the Other Plane, that the magical jargon was at best a romantic convenience and at worst obscurantism. But even so, their articles often missed the point and were both too conservative and too extravagant. You might think that to convey the full sense imagery of the swamp, some immense bandwidth would be necessary. In fact, that was not so (and if it were, the Feds would have quickly been able to spot warlock and werebot operations). A typical Portal link was around fifty thousand baud, far narrower than even a flat video channel. Mr. Slippery could feel the damp seeping through his leather boots, could feel the sweat starting on his skin even in the cold air, but this was the response of Mr. Slippery's imagination and subconscious to the cues that were actually being presented through the Portal's electrodes. The interpretation could not be arbitrary or he would be dumped back to reality and would never find the Coven; to the traveler on the Other Plane, the detail was there as long as the cues were there. And there is nothing new about this situation. Even a poor writer—if he has a sympathetic reader and an engaging plot—can evoke complete internal imagery with a few dozen words of description. The difference now is that the imagery has interactive significance, just as sensations in the real world do. Ultimately, the magic jargon was perhaps the closest fit in the vocabulary of millenium Man.

The stones were spaced more widely now, and it took all Mr. Slippery's skill to avoid falling into the noisome waters that surrounded him. Fortunately, after another hundred meters or so, the trail rose out of the water, and he was walking on shallow mud. The trees and brush grew in close around him, and large spider webs glistened across the trail and between some of the trees along the side.

Like a yo-yo from some branch high above him, a red-banded spider the size of a man's fist descended into the space right before the traveler's face. "Beware, beware," the tiny voice issued from dripping mandibles. "Beware, beware," the words were repeated, and the creature swung back and forth, nearer and farther from Mr. Slippery's face. He looked carefully at the spider's banded abdomen. There were many species of deathspider here, and each required a different response if a traveler was to survive. Finally he raised the back of his hand and held it level so that the spider could crawl onto it. The creature raced up the

damp fabric of his jacket to the open neck. There it whispered something very quietly.

Mr. Slippery listened, then grabbed the animal before it could repeat the message and threw it to the left, at the same time racing off into the tangle of webs and branches on the other side of the trail. Something heavy and wet slapped into the space where he had been, but he was already gone—racing at top speed up the incline that suddenly appeared before him.

He stopped when he reached the crest of the hill. Beyond it, he could see the solemn, massive fortress that was the Coven's haven. It was not more than five hundred meters away, illuminated as the swamp had been by a vague and indistinct light that came only partly from the sky. The trail leading down to it was much more open than the swamp had been, but the traveler proceeded as slowly as before: the sprites the warlocks set to keep eternal guard here had the nasty—though preprogrammed—habit of changing the rules in new and deadly ways.

The trail descended, then began a rocky, winding climb toward the stone and iron gates of the castle. The ground was drier here, the vegetation sparse. Leathery snapping of wings sounded above him, but Mr. Slippery knew better than to look up. Thirty meters from the moat, the heat became more than uncomfortable. He could hear the lava popping and hissing, could see occasional dollops of fire splatter up from the liquid to scorch what vegetation still lived. A pair of glowing eyes set in a coal-black head rose briefly from the moat. A second later, the rest of the creature came surging into view, cascading sparks and lava down upon the traveler. Mr. Slippery raised his hand just so, and the lethal spray separated over his head to land harmlessly on either side of him. He watched with apparent calm as the creature descended ancient stone steps to confront him.

Alan—that was the elemental's favorite name—peered nearsightedly, his head weaving faintly from side to side as he tried to recognize the traveler. "Ah, I do believe we are honored with the presence of Mr. Slippery, is it not so?" he finally said. He smiled, an open grin revealing the glowing interior of his mouth. His breath did not show flame but did have the penetrating heat of an open kiln. He rubbed his clawed hands against his asbestos T-shirt as though anxious to be proved wrong. Away from his magma moat, the dead black of his flesh lightened, trying to contain his body heat. Now he looked almost reptilian.

"Indeed it is. And come to bring my favorite little gifts." Mr. Slippery threw a leaden slug into the air and watched the elemental grab it with his mouth, his eyes slitted with pleasure—melt-in-your-mouth pleasure. They traded conversation, spells, and counterspells for several minutes. Alan's principal job was to determine that the visitor was a known member of the Coven, and he ordinarily did this with little tests of skill (the magma bath he had tried to give Mr. Slippery) and by asking the visitor questions about previous activities within the castle. Alan was a personality simulator, of course. Mr. Slippery was sure that there had never been a living operator behind that toothless, glowing smile. But he was certainly one of the best, probably the product of many hundreds of blocks of psylisp programming, and certainly superior to the little "companionship" programs you can buy nowadays, which generally become repetitive after a few hours of conversation, which don't grow, and which are unable to counter weird responses. Alan had been with the Coven and the castle since before Mr. Slippery had become a member, and no one would admit to his creation (though Wiley J. was suspected). He hadn't even had a name until this year, when Erythrina had given him that asbestos Alan Turing T-shirt.

Mr. Slippery played the game with good humor, but care. To "die" at the hands of Alan would be a painful experience that would probably wipe a lot of unbacked memory he could ill afford to lose. Such death had claimed many petitioners at this gate, folk who would not soon be seen on this plane again.

Satisfied, Alan waved a clawed fist at the watchers in the tower, and the gate—ceramic bound in wolfram clasps—was rapidly lowered for the visitor. Mr. Slippery walked quickly across, trying to ignore the spitting and bubbling that he heard below him. Alan—now all respectful—waited till he was in the castle courtyard before doing an immense belly-flop back into his magma swimming hole.

Most of the others, with the notable exception of Erythrina, had already arrived. Robin Hood, dressed in green and looking like Errol Flynn, sat across the hall in very close conversation with a remarkably good-looking female (but then they could all be remarkably good-looking here) who seemed unsure whether to project blonde or brunette. By the fireplace,

ALAN
URING

Wiley J. Bastard, the Slimey Limey, and DON.MAC were in animated discussion over a pile of maps. And in the corner, shaded from the fireplace and apparently unused, sat a classic remote printing terminal. Mr. Slippery tried to ignore that teleprinter as he crossed the hall.

"Ah, it's Slip." DON.MAC looked up from the maps and gestured him closer. "Take a look here at what the Limey has been up to."

"Hmm?" Mr. Slippery nodded at the others, then leaned over to study the top map. The margins of the paper were aging vellum, but the "map" itself hung in three dimensions, half sunk into the paper. It was a typical banking defense and cash-flow plot—that is, typical for the SIG. Most banks had no such clever ways of visualizing the automated protection of their assets. (For that matter, Mr. Slippery suspected that most banks still looked wistfully back to the days of credit cards and COBOL.) This was the sort of thing Robin Hood had developed, and it was surprising to see the Limey involved in it. He looked up questioningly. "What's the jape?"

"It's a reg'lar double-slam, Slip. Look at this careful, an' you'll see it's no ord'n'ry protection map. Seems like what you blokes call the Mafia has taken over this banking net in the Maritime states. They must be usin' Portals to do it so slick. Took me a devil of a time to figure out it was them as done it. *Ha ha!* but now that I have . . . look here, you'll see how they've been launderin' funds, embezzlin' from straight accounts.

"They're ever so clever, but not so clever as to know about Slimey." He poked a finger into the map and a trace gleamed red through the maze. "If they're lucky, they'll discover this tap next autumn, when they find themselves maybe three billion dollars short, and not a single sign of where it all disappeared to."

The others nodded. There were many covens and SIGs throughout this plane. Theirs, The Coven, was widely known, had pulled off some of the most publicized pranks of the century. Many of the others were scarcely more than social clubs. But some were old-style criminal organizations which used this plane for their own purely pragmatic and opportunistic reasons. Usually such groups weren't too difficult for the warlocks to victimize, but it was the Slimey Limey who seemed to specialize in doing so.

"But, geez, Slimey, these guys play rough, even rougher than the Great Enemy." That is, the Feds. "If they ever figure out who you really are, you'll die the True Death for sure."

"I may be slimy, but I ain't crazy. There's no way I could absorb three billion dollars—or even three million—without being discovered. But I played it like Robin over there: the money got spread around three million ordinary accounts here and in Europe, one of which just happens to be mine."

Mr. Slippery's ears perked up. "Three million accounts, you say? Each with a sudden little surplus? I'll bet I could come close to finding your True Name from that much, Slimey."

The Limey made a faffling gesture. "It's actually a wee bit more complicated. Face it, chums, none of you has ever come close to sightin' me, an' you know more than any Mafia."

That was true. They all spent a good deal of their

time in this plane trying to determine the others' True Names. It was not an empty game, for the knowledge of another's True Name effectively made him your slave—as Mr. Slippery had already discovered in an unpleasantly firsthand way. So the warlocks constantly probed one another, devised immense programs to sieve government-personnel records for the idiosyncracies that they detected in each other. At first glance, the Limey should have been one of the easiest to discover: he had plenty of mannerisms. His Brit accent was dated and broke down every so often into North American. Of all the warlocks, he was the only one neither handsome nor grotesque. His face was, in fact, so ordinary and real that Mr. Slippery had suspected that it might be his true appearance and had spent several months devising a scheme that searched secret and US and common Europe photo files for just that appearance. It had been for nothing, and they had all eventually reached the conclusion that the Limey must be doubly or triply deceptive.

Wiley J. Bastard grinned, not too impressed. "It's nice enough, and I agree that the risks are probably small, Slimey. But what do you really get? An ego boost and a little money. But we," he gestured inclusively, "are worth more than that. With a little cooperation, we could be the most powerful people in the real world. Right, DON?"

DON.MAC nodded, smirking. His face was really the only part of him that looked human or had much flexibility of expression—and even it was steely gray. The rest of DON's body was modeled after the standard Plessey-Mercedes all-weather robot.

Mr. Slippery recognized the reference. "So you're

working with the Mailman now, too, Wiley?" He glanced briefly at the teleprinter.

"Yup."

"And you still won't give us any clue what it's all about?"

Wiley shook his head. "Not unless you're serious about throwing in with us. But you all know this: DON was the first to work with the Mailman, and he's richer than Croesus now."

DON.MAC nodded again, that silly smile still on his face.

"Hmmm." It was easy to get rich. In principle, the Limey could have made three billion dollars off the Mob in his latest caper. The problem was to become that rich and avoid detection and retribution. Even Robin Hood hadn't mastered that trick—but apparently DON and Wiley thought the Mailman had done that and more. After his chat with Virginia, he was willing to believe it. Mr. Slippery turned to look more closely at the teleprinter. It was humming faintly, and as usual it had a good supply of paper. The paper was torn neatly off at the top, so that the only message visible was the Mailman's asterisk prompt. It was the only way they ever communicated with this most mysterious of their members: type a message on the device, and in an hour or a week the machine would rattle and beat, and a response of up to several thousand words would appear. In the beginning, it had not been very popular—the idea was cute, but the delays made conversation just too damn dull. He could remember seeing meters of Mailman output lying sloppily on the stone floor, mostly unread. But *now*, every one of the Mailman's golden words was

eagerly sopped up by his new apprentices, who very carefully removed every piece of output, leaving no clues for the rest of them to work with.

"Ery!" He looked toward the broad stone stairs that led down from the courtyard. It was Erythrina, the Red Witch. She swept down the stairs, her costume shimmering, now revealing, now obscuring. She had a spectacular figure and an excellent sense of design, but of course that was not what was remarkable about her. Erythrina was the sort of person who knew much more than she ever said, even though she always seemed easy to talk to. Some of her adventures—though unadvertised—were in a class with Robin Hood's. Mr. Slippery had known her well for a year; she was certainly the most interesting personality on this plane. She made him wish that all the secrets were unnecessary, that True Names could be traded as openly as phone numbers. What was she really?

Erythrina nodded to Robin Hood, then proceeded down the hall to DON.MAC, who had originally shouted greetings and now continued, "We've just been trying to convince Slimey and Slip that they are wasting their time on pranks when they could have real power and real wealth."

She glanced sharply at Wiley, who seemed strangely irritated that she had been drawn into the conversation. " 'We' meaning you and Wiley and the Mailman?"

Wiley nodded. "I just started working with them last week, Ery," as if to say, *and you can't stop me.*

"You may have something, DON. We all started out as amateurs, doing our best to make the System just a little bit uncomfortable for its bureaucratic masters. But we are experts now. We probably understand the System better than anyone on Earth. That should equate to power." It was the same thing the other two had been saying, but she could make it much more persuasive. Before his encounter with the Feds, he might have bought it (even though he always knew that the day he got serious about Coven activities and went after real gain would also be the day it ceased to be an enjoyable game and became an all-consuming job that would suck time away from the projects that made life entertaining).

Erythrina looked from Mr. Slippery to the Limey and then back. The Limey was an easygoing sort, but just now he was a bit miffed at the way his own pet project had been dismissed. "Not for me, thanky," he said shortly and began to gather up his maps.

She turned her green, faintly oriental eyes upon Mr. Slippery. "How about you, Slip? Have you signed up with the Mailman?"

He hesitated. *Maybe I should.* It seemed clear that the Mailman's confederates were being let in on at least part of his schemes. In a few hours, he might be able to learn enough to get Virginia off his back. And perhaps destroy his friends to boot; it was a hell of a bargain. *God in Heaven, why did they have to get mixed up in this? Don't they realize what the Government will do to them, if they really try to take over, if they ever try to play at being more than vandals?* "Not . . . not yet," he said finally. "I'm awfully tempted, though."

She grinned, regular white teeth flashing against her dark, faintly green face. "I, too. What do you say we talk it over, just the two of us?" She reached out a slim, dark hand to grasp his elbow. "Excuse us, gentlemen; hopefully, when we get back, you'll have a couple of new allies." And Mr. Slippery felt himself gently propelled toward the dark and musty stairs that led to Erythrina's private haunts.

Her torch burned and glowed, but there was no smoke. The flickering yellow lit their path for scant meters ahead. The stairs were steep and gently curving. He had the feeling that they must do a complete circle every few hundred steps: this was an immense spiral cut deep into the heart of the living rock. And it was alive. As the smell of mildew and rot increased, as the dripping from the ceiling grew subtly louder and the puddles in the worn steps deeper, the walls high above their heads took on shapes, and those shapes changed and flowed to follow them. Erythrina protected her part of the castle as thoroughly as the castle itself was guarded against the outside world. Mr. Slippery had no doubt that if she wished, she could trap him permanently here, along with the lizards and the rock sprites. (Of course he could always "escape" simply by falling back into the real world, but until she relented or he saw through her spells, he would not be able to access any other portion of the castle.) Working on some of their projects, he had visited her underground halls, but never anything this deep.

He watched her shapely form preceding him down, down, down. Of all the Coven (with the possible exception of Robin Hood, and of course the Mailman), she was the most powerful. He suspected that she was one of the original founders. If only there were some way of convincing her (without revealing the source of his knowledge) that the Mailman was a threat. If only there was some way of getting her cooperation in nailing down the Mailman's True Name.

Erythrina stopped short and he bumped pleasantly into her. Over her shoulder, a high door ended the passage. She moved her hand in a pattern hidden from Mr. Slippery and muttered some unlocking spell. The door split horizontally, its halves pulling apart with oiled and massive precision. Beyond, he had the impression of spots and lines of red breaking a further darkness.

"Mind your step," she said and hopped over a murky puddle that stood before the high sill of the doorway.

As the door slid shut behind them, Erythrina changed the torch to a single searing spot of white light, like some old-time incandescent bulb. The room was bright-lit now. Comfortable black leather chairs sat on black tile. Red engraving, faintly glowing, was worked into the tile and the obsidian of the walls. In contrast to the stairway, the air was fresh and clean—though still.

She waved him to a chair that faced away from the light, then sat on the edge of a broad desk. The point light glinted off her eyes, making them unreadable. Erythrina's face was slim and fine-boned, almost Asian except for the pointed ears. But the skin was dark, and her long hair had the reddish tones unique to some North American blacks. She was barely smiling now, and Mr. Slippery wished again he had some way of getting her help.

"Slip, I'm scared," she said finally, the smile gone.

You're scared! For a moment, he couldn't quite

believe his ears. "The Mailman?" he asked, hoping.

She nodded. "This is the first time in my life I've felt outgunned. I need help. Robin Hood may be the most competent, but he's basically a narcissist; I don't think I could interest him in anything beyond his immediate gratifications. That leaves you and the Limey. And I think there's something special about you. We've done a couple things together," she couldn't help herself, and grinned remembering. "They weren't real impressive, but somehow I have a feeling about you: I think you understand what things up here are silly games and what things are really important. If you think something is really important, you can be trusted to stick with it even if the going gets a little . . . bloody."

Coming from someone like Ery, the words had special meaning. It was strange, to feel both flattered and frightened. Mr. Slippery stuttered for a moment, inarticulate. "What about Wiley J? Seems to me you have special . . . influence over him."

"You knew . . . ?"

"Suspected."

"Yes, he's my thrall. Has been for almost six months. Poor Wiley turns out to be a life-insurance salesman from Peoria. Like a lot of warlocks, he's rather a Thurberesque fellow in real life: timid, always dreaming of heroic adventures and grandiose thefts. Only nowadays people like that can realize their dreams. . . . Anyway, he doesn't have the background, or the time, or the skill that I do, and I found his True Name. I enjoy the chase more than the extortion, so I haven't leaned on him too hard; now I wish I had. Since he's taken up with the Mailman, he's been giving me the

finger. Somehow Wiley thinks that what they have planned will keep him safe even if I give his True Name to the cops!"

"So the Mailman actually has some scheme for winning political power in the real world?"

She smiled. "That's what Wiley thinks. You see, poor Wiley doesn't know that there are more uses for True Names than simple blackmail. I know everything he sends over the data links, everything he has been told by the Mailman."

"So what are they up to?" It was hard to conceal his eagerness. *Perhaps this will be enough to satisfy Virginia and her goons.*

Erythrina seemed frozen for a moment, and he realized that she too must be using the low-altitude satellite net for preliminary processing: her task had just been handed off from one comsat to a nearer bird. Ordinarily it was easy to disguise the hesitation. She must be truly upset.

And when she finally replied, it wasn't really with an answer. "You know what convinced Wiley that the Mailman could deliver on his promises? It was DON.MAC—and the revolution in Venezuela. Apparently DON and the Mailman had been working on that for several months before Wiley joined them. It was to be the Mailman's first demonstration that controlling data and information services could be used to take permanent political control of a state. And Venezuela, they claimed, was perfect: it has enormous data-processing facilities—all just a bit obsolete, since they were bought when the country was at the peak of its boom time."

"But that was clearly an internal *coup*. The present leaders are local—"

"Nevertheless, DON is supposedly down there now, the real *Jefe,* for the first time in his life able to live in the physical world the way we do in this plane. If you have your own country, you are no longer small fry that must guard his True Name. You don't have to settle for crumbs."

"You said 'supposedly'."

"Slip, have you noticed anything strange about DON lately?"

Mr. Slippery thought back. DON.MAC had always been the most extreme of the werebots—after the Mailman. He was not an especially talented fellow, but he did go to great lengths to sustain the image that he was both machine and human. His persona was always present in this plane, though at least part of the time it was a simulator—like Alan out in the magma moat. The simulation was fairly good, but no one had yet produced a program that could really pass the Turing test: that is, fool a real human for any extended time. Mr. Slippery remembered the silly smile that seemed pasted on DON's face and the faintly repetitive tone of his lobbying for the Mailman. "You think the real person behind DON is gone, that we have a zombie up there?"

"Slip, I think the real DON is *dead*, and I mean the True Death."

"Maybe he just found the real world more delightful than this, now that he owns such a big hunk of it?"

"I don't think he owns anything. It's just barely possible that the Mailman had something to do with that *coup;* there are a number of coincidences between what they told Wiley beforehand and what actually happened. But I've spent a lot of time floating through the Venezuelan data bases, and I think I'd know if an outsider were on the scene, directing the new order.

"I think the Mailman is taking us on one at a time, starting with the weakest, drawing us in far enough to learn our True Names—and then destroying us. So far he has only done it to one of us. I've been watching DON.MAC both directly and automatically since the *coup,* and there has never been a real person behind that facade, not once in two thousand hours. Wiley is next. The poor slob hasn't even been told yet what country his kingdom is to be—evidence that the Mailman doesn't really have the power he claims—but even so, he's ready to do practically anything for the Mailman, and against us.

"Slip, we have *got* to identify this *thing,* this Mailman, before he can get us."

She was even more upset than Virginia and the Feds. And she was right. For the first time, he felt more afraid of the Mailman than the government agents. He held up his hands. "I'm convinced. But what should we do? You've got the best angle in Wiley. The Mailman doesn't know you've got a tap through him, does he?"

She shook her head. "Wiley is too chicken to tell him, and doesn't realize that I can do this with his True Name. But I'm already doing everything I can with that. I want to pool information, guesses, with you. Between us maybe we can see something new."

"Well for starters, it's obvious that the Mailman's

queer communication style—those long time delays—is a ploy. I know that fellow is listening all the time to what's going on in the Coven meeting hall. And he commands a number of sprites in real time." Mr. Slippery remembered the day the Mailman—or at least his teleprinter—had arrived. The image of an American Van Lines truck had pulled up at the edge of the moat, nearly intimidating Alan. The driver and loader were simulators, though good ones. They had answered all of Alan's questions correctly, then hauled the shipping crate down to the meeting hall. They hadn't left till the warlocks signed for the shipment and promised to "wire a wall outlet" for the device. This enemy definitely knew how to arouse the curiosity of his victims. Whoever controlled that printer seemed perfectly capable of normal behavior. *Perhaps it's someone we already know, like in the mysteries where the murderer masquerades as one of the victims. Robin Hood?*

"I know. In fact, he can do many things faster than I. He must control some powerful processors. But you're partly wrong: the living part of him that's behind it all really does operate with at least a one-hour turnaround time. All the quick stuff is programmed."

Mr. Slippery started to protest, then realized that she could be right. "My God, what could that mean? Why would he deliberately saddle himself with that disadvantage?"

Erythrina smiled with some satisfaction. "I'm convinced that if we knew that, we'd have this guy sighted. I agree it's too great a disadvantage to be a simple red herring. I think he must have some time-delay problem to begin with, and—"

"—and he has exaggerated it?" But even if the Mailman were an Australian, the low satellite net made delays so short that he would probably be indistinguishable from a European or a Japanese. There was no place on Earth where . . . *but there are places off Earth!* The mass-transmit satellites were in synchronous orbit 120 milliseconds out. There were about two hundred people there. And further out, at L5, there were at least another four hundred. Some were near-permanent residents. A strange idea, but still a possibility.

"*I* don't think he has exaggerated. Slip, I think the Mailman—not his processors and simulators, you understand—is at least a half-hour out from Earth, probably in the asteroid belt."

She smiled suddenly, and Mr. Slippery realized that his jaw must be resting on his chest. Except for the Joint Mars Recon, no human had been anywhere near that far out. *No human.* Mr. Slippery felt his ordinary, everyday world disintegrating into sheer science fiction. This was ridiculous.

"I know you don't believe; it took me a while to. He's not so obvious that he doesn't add in some time delay to disguise the cyclic variation in our relative positions. But it *is* a consistent explanation for the delay. These last few weeks I've been sniffing around the classified reports on our asteroid probes; there are definitely some mysterious things out there."

"Okay. It's consistent. But you're talking about an interstellar *invasion*. Even if NASA had the funding, it would take them decades to put the smallest interstellar probe together—and decades more for the flight. Trying to invade anyone with those logistics would be impossible. And if these aliens have a decent stardrive, why do they bother with deception? They could just move in and brush us aside."

"Ah, that's the point, Slip. The invasion I'm thinking of doesn't need any "stardrive," and it works fine against any race at exactly our point of development. Right: most likely interstellar war is a fantastically expensive business, with decade lead times. What better policy for an imperialistic, highly technological race than to lie doggo listening for evidence of younger civilizations? When they detect such, they send only one ship. When it arrives in the victims' solar system, the Computer Age is in full bloom there. We in the Coven know how fragile the present system is; it is only fear of exposure that prevents some warlocks from trying to take over. Just think how appealing our naïveté must be to an older civilization that has thousands of years of experience at managing data systems. Their small crew of agents moves in as close as local military surveillance permits and gradually insinuates itself into the victims' system. They eliminate what sharp individuals they detect in that system—people like us—and then they go after the bureaucracies and the military. In ten or twenty years, another fiefdom is ready for the arrival of the master race."

She lapsed into silence, and for a long moment they stared at each other. It did all hang together with a weird sort of logic. "What can we do, then?"

"That's the question." She shook her head sadly, came across the room to sit beside him. Now that she had said her piece, the fire had gone out of her. For the first time since he had known her, Erythrina looked depressed. "We could just forsake this plane and stay in the real world. The Mailman might still be able to track us down, but we'd be of no more interest to him than anyone else. If we were lucky, we might have years before he takes over." She straightened. "I'll tell you this: if we want to live as warlocks, we have to stop him soon—within days at most. After he gets Wiley, he may drop the con tactics for something more direct.

"If I'm right about the Mailman, then our best bet would be to discover his communication link. That would be his Achilles' heel; there's no way you can hide in the crowd when you're beaming from that far away. We've got to take some real chances now, do things we'd never risk before. I figure that if we work together, maybe we can lessen the risk that either of us is identified."

He nodded. Ordinarily a prudent warlock used only limited bandwidth and so was confined to a kind of linear, personal perception. If they grabbed a few hundred megahertz of comm space, and a bigger share of rented processors, they could manipulate and search files in a way that would boggle Virginia the femcop. Of course, they would be much more easily identifiable. With two of them, though, they might be able to keep it up safely for a brief time, confusing the government and the Mailman with a multiplicity of clues. "Frankly, I don't buy the alien part. But the rest of what you say makes sense, and that's what counts. Like you say, we're going to have to take some chances."

TRUE NAMES

"Right!" She smiled and reached behind his neck to draw his face to hers. She was a very good kisser. (Not everyone was. It was one thing just to look gorgeous, and another to project and respond to the many sensory cues in something as interactive as kissing.) He was just warming to this exercise of their mutual abilities when she broke off. "And the best time to start is right now. The others think we're sealed away down here. If strange things happen during the next few hours, it's less likely the Mailman will suspect *us*." She reached up to catch the light point in her hand. For an instant, blades of harsh white slipped out from between her fingers; then all was dark. He felt faint air motion as her hands moved through another spell. There were words, distorted and unidentifiable. Then the light was back, but as a torch again, and a door—a second door—had opened in the far wall.

He followed her up the passage that stretched straight and gently rising as far as the torchlight shone. They were walking a path that could not be—or at least that no one in the Coven could have believed. The castle was basically a logical structure "fleshed" out with the sensory cues that allowed the warlocks to move about it as one would a physical structure. Its moats and walls were part of that logical structure, and though they had no physical reality outside of the varying potentials in whatever processors were running the program, they were proof against the movement of the equally "unreal" perceptions of the inhabitants of the plane. Erythrina and Mr. Slippery could have escaped the deep room simply by falling back into the real world, but in doing so, they would have left a chain of unclosed processor links. Their departure would have been detected by every Coven member, even by Alan, even by the sprites. An orderly departure scheme, such as represented by this tunnel, could only mean that Erythrina was far too clever to need his help, or that she had been one of the original builders of the castle some four years earlier (lost in the Mists of Time, as the Limey put it).

They were wild dogs now, large enough so as not likely to be bothered, small enough to be mistaken for the amateur users that are seen more and more in the Other Plane as the price of Portals declines and the skill of the public increases. Mr. Slippery followed Erythrina down narrow paths, deeper and deeper into the swamp that represented commercial and government data space. Occasionally he was aware of sprites or simulators watching them with hostile eyes from nests off to the sides of the trail. These were idle creations in many cases—program units designed to infuriate or amuse later visitors to the plane. But many of them guarded information caches, or peepholes into other folks' affairs, or meeting places of other SIGs. The Coven might be the most sophisticated group of users on this plane, but they were far from being alone.

The brush got taller, bending over the trail to drip on their backs. But the water was clear here, spread in quiet ponds on either side of their path. Light came from the water itself, a pearly luminescence that shone upward on the trunks of the waterbound trees and sparkled faintly in the droplets of water in their moss and leaves. That light was the representation of the really huge data bases run by the government and the largest companies. It did not correspond to a specific geographical location, but rather to the main East/West net that stretches through selected installations from Honolulu to Oxford, taking advantage of the time zones to spread the user load.

"Just a little bit farther," Erythrina said over her shoulder, speaking in the beast language (encipherment) that they had chosen with their forms.

Minutes later, they shrank into the brush, out of the way of two armored hackers that proceeded implacably up the trail. The pair drove in single file, the impossibly large eight-cylinder engines on their bikes belching fire and smoke and noise. The one bringing up the rear carried an old-style recoilless rifle decorated with swastikas and chrome. Dim fires glowed through their blackened face plates. The two dogs eyed the bikers timidly, as befitted their present disguise, but Mr. Slippery had the feeling he was looking at a couple of amateurs who were imaging beyond their station in life: the bikes' tires didn't always touch the ground, and the tracks they left didn't quite match the texture of the muck. Anyone could put on a heroic image in this plane, or appear as some dreadful monster. The problem was that there were always skilled users who were willing to cut such pretenders down to size—perhaps even to destroy their access. It befitted the less experienced to appear small and inconspicuous, and to stay out of others' way.

(Mr. Slippery had often speculated just how the simple notion of using high-resolution EEGs as input/output devices had caused the development of the "magical world" representation of data space. The Limey and Erythrina argued that sprites, reincarnation, spells, and castles were the natural tools here, more natural than the atomistic twentieth-century notions of data structures, programs, files, and communications protocols. It was, they argued, just more convenient for the mind to use the global ideas of magic as the tokens to manipulate this new environment. They had a point; in fact, it was likely that the governments of the world hadn't caught up to the skills of the better warlocks simply because they refused to indulge in the foolish imaginings of fantasy. Mr. Slippery looked down at the reflection in the pool beside him and saw the huge canine face and lolling tongue looking up at him; he winked at the image. He knew that despite all his friends' high intellectual arguments, there was another reason for the present state of affairs, a reason that went back to the Moon Lander and Adventure games at the "dawn of time": it was simply a hell of a lot of fun to live in a world as malleable as the human imagination.)

Once the riders were out of sight, Erythrina moved back across the path to the edge of the pond and peered long and hard down between the lilies, into the limpid depths. "Okay, let's do some cross-correlation. You take the JPL data base, and I'll take the Harvard Multispectral Patrol. Start with data coming off space probes out to ten AUs. I have a suspicion the easiest way for the Mailman to disguise his transmissions is to play trojan horse with data from a NASA spacecraft."

Mr. Slippery nodded. One way or another, they should resolve her alien invasion theory first.

"It should take me about half an hour to get in place. After that, we can set up for the correlation. Hmmm . . . if something goes wrong, let's agree to meet at Mass Transmit 3," and she gave a password scheme. Clearly that would be an emergency situation. If they weren't back in the castle within three or four hours, the others would certainly guess the existence of her secret exit.

Erythrina tensed, then dived into the water. There was a small splash, and the lilies bobbed gently in the expanding ring waves. Mr. Slippery looked deep, but as expected, there was no further sign of her. He padded around the side of the pool, trying to identify the special glow of the JPL data base.

There was thrashing near one of the larger lilies, one that he recognized as obscuring the NSA connections with the East/West net. A large bullfrog scrambled out of the water onto the pad and turned to look at him. "Aha! Gotcha, you sonofabitch!"

It was Virginia; the voice was the same, even if the body was different. *"Shhhhhh!"* said Mr. Slippery, and looked wildly about for signs of eavesdroppers. There were none, but that did not mean they were safe. He spread his best privacy spell over her and crawled to the point closest to the lily. They sat glaring at each other like some characters out of La Fontaine: The Tale of the Frog and Dog. How dearly he would love to leap across the water and bite off that fat little head. Unfortunately the victory would be a bit temporary. "How did you find me?" Mr. Slippery growled. If people as inexperienced as the Feds could trace him down in his disguise, he was hardly safe from the Mailman.

"You forget," the frog puffed smugly. "We know your Name. It's simple to monitor your home processor and follow your every move."

Mr. Slippery whined deep in his throat. *In thrall to a frog. Even Wiley has done better than that.* "Okay, so you found me. Now what do you want?"

"To let you know that we want results, and to get a progress report."

He lowered his muzzle till his eyes were even with Virginia's. "Heh heh. I'll give you a progress report, but you're not going to like it." And he proceeded to explain Erythrina's theory that the Mailman was an alien invasion.

"Rubbish," spoke the frog afterward. "Sheer fantasy! You're going to have to do better than that, Pol—er, Mister."

He shuddered. She had almost spoken his Name. Was that a calculated threat or was she simply as stupid as she seemed? Nevertheless, he persisted. "Well then, what about Venezuela?" He related the evidence Ery had that the *coup* in that country was the Mailman's work.

This time the frog did not reply. Its eyes glazed over with apparent shock, and he realized that Virginia must be consulting people at the other end. Almost fifteen minutes passed. When the frog's eyes cleared, it was much more subdued. "We'll check on that one. What you say is possible. Just barely possible. If true . . . well, if it's true, this is the biggest threat we've had to face this century."

And you see that I am perhaps the only one who can bail you out. Mr. Slippery relaxed slightly. If they only realized it, they were thralled to him as much as

Vernor Vinge

the reverse—at least for the moment. Then he remembered Erythrina's plan to grab as much power as they could for a brief time and try to use that advantage to flush the Mailman out. With the Feds on their side, they could do more than Ery had ever imagined. He said as much to Virginia.

The frog croaked, "*You* . . . want . . . *us* . . . to give you carte blanche in the Federal data system? Maybe you'd like to be President and Chair of the JCS, to boot?"

"Hey, that's not what I said. I know it's an extraordinary suggestion, but this is an extraordinary situation. And in any case, you know my Name. There's no way I can get around that."

The frog went glassy-eyed again, but this time for only a couple of minutes. "We'll get back to you on that. We've got a lot of checking to do on the rest of your theories before we commit ourselves to anything. Till further notice, though, you're grounded."

"Wait!" What would Ery do when he didn't show? If he wasn't back in the castle in three or four hours, the others would surely know about the secret exit.

The frog was implacable. "I said, you're grounded, Mister. We want you back in the real world immediately. And you'll stay grounded till you hear from us. Got it?"

The dog slumped. "Yeah."

"Okay." The frog clambered heavily to the edge of the sagging lily and dumped itself ungracefully into the water. After a few seconds, Mr. Slippery followed.

Coming back was much like waking from a deep daydream; only here it was the middle of the night.

Roger Pollack stood, stretching, trying to get the

kinks out of his muscles. Almost four hours he had been gone, longer than ever before. Normally his concentration began to fail after two or three hours. Since he didn't like the thought of drugging up, this put a definite limit on his endurance in the Other Plane.

Beyond the bungalow's picture window, the pines stood silhouetted against the Milky Way. He cranked open a pane and listened to the night birds trilling out there in the trees. It was near the end of spring; he liked to imagine he could see dim polar twilight to the north. More likely it was just Crescent City. Pollack leaned close to the window and looked high into the sky, where Mars sat close to Jupiter. It was hard to think of a threat to his own life from as far away as that.

Pollack backed up the spells acquired during this last session, powered down his system, and stumbled off to bed.

The following morning and afternoon seemed the longest of Roger Pollack's life. How would they get in touch with him? Another visit of goons and black Lincolns? What had Erythrina done when he didn't make contact? Was she all right?

And there was just no way of checking. He paced back and forth across his tiny living room, the novel-plots that were his normal work forgotten. *Ah, but there is a way.* He looked at his old data set with dawning recognition. Virginia had said to stay out of the Other Plane. But how could they object to his using a simple data set, no more efficient than millions used by office workers all over the world?

He sat down at the set, scraped the dust from the handpads and screen. He awkwardly entered long-unused call symbols and watched the flow of news across the screen. A few queries and he discovered that no great disasters had occurred overnight, that the insurgency in Indonesia seemed temporarily abated. (Wiley J. was not to be king just yet.) There were no reports of big-time data vandals biting the dust.

Pollack grunted. He had forgotten how tedious it was to see the world through a data set, even with audio entry. In the Other Plane, he could pick up this sort of information in seconds, as casually as an ordinary mortal might glance out the window to see if it is raining. He dumped the last twenty-four hours of the world bulletin board into his home memory space and began checking through it. The bulletin board was ideal for untraceable reception of messages: anyone on Earth could leave a message—indexed by subject, target audience, and source. If a user copied the entire board, and *then* searched it, there was no outside record of exactly what information he was interested in. There were also simple ways to make nearly untraceable entries on the board.

As usual, there were about a dozen messages for Mr. Slippery. Most of them were from fans; the Coven had greater notoriety than any other vandal SIG. A few were for other Mr. Slipperys. With five billion people in the world, that wasn't surprising.

And one of the memos was from the Mailman; that's what it said in the source field. Pollack punched the message up on the screen. It was in caps, with no color or sound. Like all messages directly from the

Mailman, it looked as if it came off some incredibly ancient I/O device:

> YOU COULD HAVE BEEN RICH. YOU COULD HAVE RULED. INSTEAD YOU CONSPIRED AGAINST ME. I KNOW ABOUT THE SECRET EXIT. I KNOW ABOUT YOUR DOGGY DEPARTURE. YOU AND THE RED ONE ARE DEAD NOW. IF YOU EVER SNEAK BACK ONTO THIS PLANE, IT WILL BE THE TRUE DEATH—I AM THAT CLOSE TO KNOWING YOUR NAMES.
> *****WATCH FOR ME IN THE NEWS,
> SUCKER*********

Bluff, thought Roger. *He wouldn't be sending out warnings if he has that kind of power*. Still, there was a dropping sensation in his stomach. The Mailman shouldn't have known about the dog disguise. Was he onto Mr. Slippery's connection with the Feds? If so, he might really be able to find Slippery's True Name. And what sort of danger was Ery in? What had she done when he missed the rendezvous at Mass Transmit 3?

A quick search showed no messages from Erythrina. Either she was looking for him in the Other Plane, or she was as thoroughly grounded as he.

He was still stewing on this when the phone rang. He said, "Accept, no video send." His data set cleared to an even gray: the caller was not sending video either.

"You're still there? Good." It was Virginia. Her voice sounded a bit odd, subdued and tense. Perhaps it was just the effect of the scrambling algorithms. He prayed she would not trust that scrambling. He had never bothered to make his phone any more secure than average. (And he had seen the schemes Wiley J. and Robin Hood had devised to decrypt thousands of commercial phone messages in real-time and monitor for key phrases, signaling them when anything interesting was detected. They couldn't use the technique very effectively, since it took an enormous amount of processor space, but the Mailman was probably not so limited.)

Virginia continued, "No names, okay? We checked out what you told us and . . . it looks like you're right. We can't be sure about your theory about *his* origin, but what you said about the international situation was verified." So the Venezuela *coup* had been an outside take-over. "Furthermore, we think *he* has infiltrated us much more than we thought. It may be that the evidence we had of unsuccessful meddling was just a red herring." Pollack recognized the fear in her voice now. Apparently the Feds saw that they were up against something catastrophic. They were caught with their countermeasures down, and their only hope lay with unreliables like Pollack.

"Anyway, we're going ahead with what you suggested. We'll provide you two with the resources you requested. We want you in the Other . . . place as soon as possible. We can talk more there."

"I'm on my way. I'll check with my friend and get back to you there." He cut the connection without waiting for a reply. Pollack sat back, trying to savor this triumph and the near-pleading in the cop's voice. Somehow, he couldn't. He knew what a hard case she was; anything that could make her crawl was more hellish than anything he wanted to face.

His first stop was Mass Transmit 3. Physically, MT3 was a two-thousand-tonne satellite in synchronous orbit over the Indian Ocean. The Mass Transmits handled most of the planet's noninteractive communications (and in fact that included a lot of transmission that most people regarded as interactive—such as human/human and the simpler human/computer conversations). Bandwidth and processor space was cheaper on the Mass Transmits because of the 240- to 900-millisecond time delays that were involved.

As such, it was a nice out-of-the-way meeting place, and in the Other Plane it was represented as a five-meter-wide ledge near the top of a mountain that rose from the forests and swamps that stood for the lower satellite layer and the ground-based nets. In the distance were two similar peaks, clear in pale sky.

Mr. Slippery leaned out into the chill breeze that swept the face of the mountain and looked down past the timberline, past the evergreen forests. Through the unnatural mists that blanketed those realms, he thought he could see the Coven's castle.

Perhaps he should go there, or down to the swamps. There was no sign of Erythrina. Only sprites in the forms of bats and tiny griffins were to be seen here. They sailed back and forth over him, sometimes soaring far higher, toward the uttermost peak itself.

Mr. Slippery himself was in an extravagant winged man form, one that subtly projected amateurism, one that he hoped would pass the inspection of the enemy's eyes and ears. He fluttered clumsily across the ledge toward a small cave that provided some shelter from the whistling wind. Fine, wind-dropped snow lay in a small bank before the entrance. The insects he found in the cave were no more than what they seemed—amateur transponders.

He turned and started back toward the drop-off; he was going to have to face this alone. But as he passed the snowbank, the wind swirled it up and tiny crystals stung his face and hands and nose. *Trap!* He jumped backward, his fastest escape spell coming to his lips, at the same time cursing himself for not establishing the spell before. The time delay was just too long; the trap lived here at MT3 and could react faster than he. The little snow-devil dragged the crystals up into a swirling column of singing motes that chimed in near-unison, "W-w-wait-t-t!"

The sound matched deep-set recognition patterns; this was Erythrina's work. Three hundred milliseconds passed, and the wind suddenly picked up the rest of the snow and whirled into a more substantial, taller column. Mr. Slippery realized that the trap had been more of an alarm, set to bring Ery if he should be recognized here. But her arrival was so quick that she must already have been at work somewhere in this plane.

"Where have you been-n-n!" The snow-devil's chime was a combination of rage and concern.

Mr. Slippery threw a second spell over the one he recognized she had cast. There was no help for it: he would have to tell her that the Feds had his Name. And with that news, Virginia's confirmation about Venezuela and the Feds' offer to help.

Erythrina didn't respond immediately—and only part

of the delay was light lag. Then the swirling snow flecks that represented her gusted up around him. "So you lose no matter how this comes out, eh? I'm sorry, Slip."

Mr. Slippery's wings drooped. "Yeah. But I'm beginning to believe it will be the True Death for us all if we don't stop the Mailman. He really means to take over . . . everything. Can you imagine what it would be like if all the governments' wee megalomaniacs got replaced by one big one?"

The usual pause. The snow-devil seemed to shudder in on itself. "You're right; we've got to stop him even if it means working for Sammy Sugar and the entire DoW." She chuckled, a near-inaudible chiming. "Even if it means that *they* have to work for *us*." She could laugh; the Feds didn't know her Name. "How did your Federal Friends say we could plug into their system?" Her form was changing again—to a solid, winged form, an albino eagle. The only red she allowed herself was in the eyes, which gleamed with inner light.

"At the Laurel end of the old arpa net. We'll get something near carte blanche on that and on the DoJ domestic intelligence files, but we have to enter through one physical location and with just the password scheme they specify." He and Erythrina would have more power than any vandals in history, but they would be on a short leash, nevertheless.

His wings beat briefly, and he rose into the air. After the usual pause, the eagle followed. They flew almost to the mountain's peak, then began the long, slow glide toward the marshes below, the chill air whistling around them. In principle, they could have made the transfer to the Laurel terminus virtually instantaneously. But it was not mere romanticism that made them move so cautiously—as many a novice had discovered the hard way. What appeared to the conscious mind as a search for air currents and clear lanes through the scattered clouds was a manifestation of the almost-subconscious working of programs that gradually transferred processing from rented space on MT3 to low satellite and ground-based stations. The game was tricky and time-consuming, but it made it virtually impossible for others to trace their origin. The greatest danger of detection would probably occur at Laurel, where they would be forced to access the system through a single input device.

The sky glowed momentarily; seconds passed, and an airborne fist slammed into them from behind. The shock wave sent them tumbling tail over wing toward the forests below. Mr. Slippery straightened his chaotic flailing into a head-first dive. Looking back—which was easy to do in his present attitude—he saw the peak that had been MT3 glowing red, steam rising over descending avalanches of lava. Even at this distance, he could see tiny motes swirling above the inferno. (Attackers looking for the prey that had fled?) Had it come just a few seconds earlier, they would have had most of their processing still locked into MT3 and the disaster—whatever it really was—would have knocked them out of this plane. It wouldn't have been the True Death, but it might well have grounded them for days.

On his right, he glimpsed the white eagle in a controlled dive; they had had just enough communi-

cations established off MT3 to survive. As they fell deeper into the humid air of the lowlands, Mr. Slippery dipped into the news channels: word was already coming over the *LA Times* of the fluke accident in which the Hokkaido aerospace launching laser had somehow shone on MT3's optics. The laser had shone for microseconds and at reduced power; the damage had been nothing like a Finger of God, say. No one had been hurt, but wideband communications would be down for some time, and several hundred million dollars of information traffic was stalled. There would be investigations and a lot of very irate customers.

It had been no accident, Mr. Slippery was sure. The Mailman was showing his teeth, revealing infiltration no one had suspected. He must guess what his opponents were up to.

They leveled out a dozen meters above the pine forest that bordered the swamps. The air around them was thick and humid, and the faraway mountains were almost invisible. Clouds had moved in, and a storm was on the way. They were now securely locked into the low-level satellite net, but thousands of new users were clamoring for entry, too. The loss of MT3 would make the Other Plane a turbulent place for several weeks, as heavy users tried to shift their traffic here.

He swooped low over the swamp, searching for the one particular pond with the one particularly large water lily that marked the only entrance Virginia would permit them. There! He banked off to the side, Erythrina following, and looked for signs of the Mailman or his friends in the mucky clearings that surrounded the pond.

But there was little purpose in further caution. Flying about like this, they would be clearly visible to any ambushers waiting by the pond. *Better to move fast now that we're committed.* He signaled the red-eyed eagle, and they dived toward the placid water. That surface marked the symbolic transition to observation mode. No longer was he aware of a winged form or of water coming up and around him. Now he was interacting directly with the I/O protocols of a computing center in the vicinity of Laurel, Maryland. He sensed Ery poking around on her own. This wasn't the arpa entrance. He slipped "sideways" into an old-fashioned government office complex. The "feel" of the 1990-style data sets was unmistakable. He was fleetingly aware of memos written and edited, reports hauled in and out of storage. One of the vandals' favorite sports—and one that even the moderately skilled could indulge in—was to infiltrate one of these office complexes and simulate higher level input to make absurd and impossible demands on the local staff.

This was not the time for such games, and this was still not the entrance. He pulled away from the office complex and searched through some old directories. Arpa went back more than half a century, the first of the serious data nets, now (figuratively) gathering dust. The number was still there, though. He signaled Erythrina, and the two of them presented themselves at the log-in point and provided just the codes that Virginia had given him.

. . . and they were in. They eagerly soaked in the

megabytes of password keys and access data that Virginia's people had left there. At the same time, they were aware that this activity was being monitored. The Feds were taking an immense chance leaving this material here, and they were going to do their best to keep a rein on their temporary vandal allies.

In fifteen seconds, they had learned more about the inner workings of the Justice Department and DoW than the Coven had in fifteen months. Mr. Slippery guessed that Erythrina must be busy plotting what she would do with all that data later on. For him, of course, there was no future in it. They drifted out of the arpa "vault" into the larger data spaces that were the Department of Justice files. He could see that there was nothing hidden from them; random archive retrievals were all being honored and with a speed that would have made deception impossible. They had subpoena power and clearances and more.

"Let's go get 'im, Slip." Erythrina's voice seemed hollow and inhuman in this underimaged realm. (How long would it be before the Feds started to make their data perceivable analogically, as on the Other Plane? It might be a little undignified, but it would revolutionize their operation—which, from the Coven's standpoint, might be quite a bad thing.)

Mr. Slippery "nodded." Now they had more than enough power to undertake the sort of work they had planned. In seconds, they had searched all the locally available files on off-planet transmissions. Then they dove out of the DoJ net, Mr. Slippery to Pasadena and the JPL planetary probe archives, Erythrina to Cambridge and the Harvard Multispectral Patrol.

It should take several hours to survey these records, to determine just what transmissions might be cover for the alien invasion that both the Feds and Erythrina were guessing had begun. But Mr. Slippery had barely started when he noticed that there were dozens of processors within reach that he could just grab with his new Federal powers. He checked carefully to make sure he wasn't upsetting air traffic control or hospital life support, then quietly stole the computing resources of several hundred unknowing users, whose data sets automatically switched to other resources. Now he had more power than he ever would have risked taking in the past. On the other side of the continent, he was aware that Erythrina had done something similar.

In three minutes, they had sifted through five years' transmissions far more thoroughly than they had originally planned.

"No sign of him," he sighed and "looked" at Erythrina. They had found plenty of irregular sources at Harvard, but there was no orbital fit. All transmissions from the NASA probes checked out legitimately.

"Yes." Her face, with its dark skin and slanting eyes, seemed to hover beside him. Apparently with her new power, she could image even here. "But you know, we haven't really done much more than the Feds could—given a couple months of data set work. . . . I know, it's more than we had planned to do. But we've barely used the resources they've opened to us."

It was true. He looked around, feeling suddenly like a small boy let loose in a candy shop: he sensed enormous data bases and the power that would let him use them. Perhaps the cops had not intended them to take advantage of this, but it was obvious that with these powers, they could do a search no enemy could evade. "Okay," he said finally, "let's pig it."

Ery laughed and made a loud snuffling sound. Carefully, quickly, they grabbed noncritical data-processing facilities along all the East/West nets. In seconds, they were the biggest users in North America. The drain would be clear to anyone monitoring the System, though a casual user might notice only increased delays in turnaround. Modern nets are at least as resilient as old-time power nets—but like power nets, they have their elastic limit and their breaking point. So far, at least, he and Erythrina were far short of those.

—but they were experiencing what no human had ever known before, a sensory bandwidth thousands of times normal. For seconds that seemed without end, their minds were filled with a jumble verging on pain, data that was not information and information that was not knowledge. To hear ten million simultaneous phone conversations, to see the continent's entire video output, should have been a white noise. Instead it was a tidal wave of detail rammed through the tiny aperture of their minds. The pain increased, and Mr. Slippery panicked. This could be the True Death, some kind of sensory burnout—

Erythrina's voice was faint against the roar, "*Use everything, not just the inputs!*" And he had just enough sense left to see what she meant. He controlled more than raw data now; if he could master them, the continent's computers could process this avalanche, much the way parts of the human brain preprocess their input. More seconds passed, but now with a sense of time, as he struggled to distribute his very consciousness through the System.

Then it was over, and he had control once more. But things would never be the same: the human that had been Mr. Slippery was an insect wandering in the cathedral his mind had become. There simply was more there than before. No sparrow could fall without his knowledge, via air traffic control; no check could be cashed without his noticing over the bank communication net. More than three hundred million lives swept before what his senses had become.

Around and through him, he felt the other occupant—Erythrina, now equally grown. They looked at each other for an unending fraction of a second, their communication more kinesthetic than verbal. Finally she smiled, the old smile now deep with meanings she could never image before. "Pity the poor Mailman now!"

Again they searched, but now it was through all the civil data bases, a search that could only be dreamed of by mortals. The signs were there, a near invisible system of manipulations hidden among more routine crimes and vandalisms. Someone had been at work within the Venezuelan system, at least at the North American end. The trail was tricky to follow—their enemy seemed to have at least some of their own powers—but they saw it lead back into the labyrinths of the Federal bureaucracy: resources diverted, individuals promoted or transferred, not quite according to the automatic regulations that should govern. These were changes so small they were never guessed at by ordinary employees and only just sensed by the cops. But over the months, they added up to an instability that neither of the two searchers could quite understand except to know that it was planned and that it did the status quo no good.

"He's still too sharp for us, Slip. We're all over the civil nets and we haven't seen any living sign of him; yet we know he does heavy processing on Earth or in low orbit."

"So he's either off North America, or else he has penetrated the . . . military."

"I bet it's a little of both. The point is, we're going to have to follow him."

And that meant taking over at least part of the US military system. Even if that was possible, it certainly went far beyond what Virginia and her friends had intended. As far as the cops were concerned, it would mean that the threat against the government was tripled. So far he hadn't detected any objections to their searching, but he was aware of Virginia and her superiors deep in some kind of bunker at Langley, intently watching a whole wall full of monitors, trying to figure out just what he was up to and if it was time to pull the plug on him.

Erythrina was aware of his objections almost as fast as he could bring them to mind. "We don't have any choice, Slip. We have to take control. The Feds aren't the only thing watching us. If we don't get the Mailman on this try, he is sure as hell going to get us."

That was easy for her to say. None of her enemies yet knew her True Name. Mr. Slippery had somehow to survive *two* enemies. On the other hand, he suspected that the deadlier of those enemies was the Mailman. "Only one way to go and that's up, huh? Okay, I'll play."

They settled into a game that was familiar now, grabbing more and more computing facilities, but now from common Europe and Asia. At the same time, they attacked the harder problem—infiltrating the various North American military nets. Both projects were beyond normal humans or any group of normal humans, but by now their powers were greater than any single civil entity in the world.

The foreign data centers yielded easily, scarcely more than minutes' work. The military was a different story. The Feds had spent many years and hundreds of billions of dollars to make the military command and control system secure. But they had not counted on the attack from all directions that they faced now; in moments more, the two searchers found themselves on the inside of the NSA control system—

—and under attack! Impressions of a dozen sleek, deadly forms converging on them, and sudden loss of control over many of the processors he depended on. He and Erythrina flailed out wildly, clumsy giants hacking at fast-moving hawks. There was imagery here, as detailed as on the Other Plane. They were fighting people with some of the skills the warlocks had developed—and a lot more power. But it was still an uneven contest. He and Erythrina had too much experience and too much sheer processing mass behind them. One by one, the fighters flashed into incandescent destruction.

He realized almost instantly that these were not

the Mailman's tools. They were powerful, but they fought as only moderately skilled warlocks might. In fact, they had encountered the most secret defense the government had for its military command and control. The civilian bureaucracies had stuck with obsolete data sets and old-fashioned dp languages, but the cutting edge of the military is always more willing to experiment. They had developed something like the warlocks' system. Perhaps they didn't use magical jargon to describe their computer/human symbiosis, but the techniques and the attitudes were the same. These swift-moving fighters flew against a background imagery that was like an olive drab Other Plane.

Compared to his present power, they were nothing. Even as he and Erythrina swept the defenders out of the "sky," he could feel his consciousness expanding further as more and more of the military system was absorbed into their pattern. Every piece of space junk out to one million kilometers floated in crystal detail before his attention; in a fraction of a second he sorted through it all, searching for some evidence of alien intelligence. No sign of the Mailman.

The military and diplomatic communications of the preceding fifty years showed before the light of their minds. At the same time as they surveyed the satellite data, Mr. Slippery and Erythrina swept through these bureaucratic communications, looking carefully but with flickering speed at every requisition for toilet paper, every "declaration" of secret war, every travel voucher, every one of the trillions of pieces of "paper" that made it possible for the machinery of state to creak forward. And here the signs were much clearer:

large sections were subtly changed, giving the same feeling the eye's blind spot gives, the feeling that nothing is really obscured but that some things are simply gone. Some of the distortions were immense. Under their microscopic yet global scrutiny, it was obvious that all of Venezuela, large parts of Alaska, and most of the economic base for the low satellite net were all controlled by some single interest that had little connection with the proper owners. Who their enemy was was still a mystery, but his works loomed larger and larger around them.

In a distant corner of what his mind had become, tiny insects buzzed with homicidal fury, tiny insects who knew Mr. Slippery's True Name. They knew what he and Erythrina had done, and right now they were more scared of the two warlocks than they had ever been of the Mailman. As he and Ery continued their search, he listened to the signals coming from the Langley command post, followed the helicopter gunships that were dispatched toward a single rural bungalow in Northern California—and changed their encrypted commands so that the sortie dumped its load of death on an uninhabited stretch of the Pacific.

Still with a tiny fraction of his attention, Mr. Slippery noticed that Virginia—actually her superiors, who had long since taken over the operation—knew of this defense. They were still receiving real-time pictures from military satellites.

He signaled a pause to Erythrina. For a few seconds, she would work alone while he dealt with these persistent antagonists. He felt like a man attacked by several puppies: they were annoying and could cause substantial damage unless he took more trouble than they were worth. They had to be stopped without causing themselves injury.

He should freeze the West Coast military and any launch complexes that could reach his body. Beyond that, it would be a good idea to block recon satellite transmission of the California area. And of course, he'd better deal with the Finger of God installations that were above the California horizon. Already he felt one of those heavy lasers, sweeping along in its ten-thousand-kilometer orbit, go into aiming mode and begin charging. He still had plenty of time—at least two or three seconds—before the weapons laser reached its lowest discharge threshold. Still, this was the most immediate threat. Mr. Slippery sent a tendril of consciousness into the tiny processor aboard the Finger of God satellite—

—and withdrew, bloodied. *Someone was already there*. Not Erythrina and not the little military warlocks. *Someone* too great for even him to overpower.

"*Ery!* I've found him!" It came out a scream. The laser's bore was centered on a spot thousands of kilometers below, a tiny house that in less than a second would become an expanding ball of plasma at the end of a columnar explosion descending through the atmosphere.

Over and over in that last second, Mr. Slippery threw himself against the barrier he felt around the tiny military processor—with no success. He traced its control to the lower satellite net, to bigger processors that were equally shielded. Now he had a feel for the nature of his opponent. It was not the direct imagery he was used to on the Other Plane; this was more like fighting blindfolded. He could sense the other's style. The enemy was not revealing any more of himself than was necessary to keep control of the Finger of God for another few hundred milliseconds.

Mr. Slippery slashed, trying to cut the enemy's communications. But his opponent was strong, much stronger—he now realized—than himself. He was vaguely aware of the other's connections to the computing power in those blind-spot areas he and Erythrina had discovered. But for all that power, he was almost the enemy's equal. There was something missing from the other, some critical element of imagination or originality. If Erythrina would only come, they might be able to stop him. Milliseconds separated him from the True Death. He looked desperately around. *Where is she?*

Military Status announced the discharge of an Orbital Weapons Laser. He cowered even as his quickened perceptions counted the microseconds that remained till his certain destruction, even as he noticed a ball of glowing plasma expanding about what had been a Finger of God—*the Finger that had been aimed at him!*

He could see now what had happened. While he and the other had been fighting, Erythrina had commandeered another of the weapons satellites, one already very near discharge threshold, and destroyed the threat to him.

Even as he realized this, the enemy was on him again, this time attacking conventionally, trying to destroy Mr. Slippery's communications and processing space. But now that enemy had to fight both Erythrina and Mr. Slippery. The other's lack of imagination and creativity was beginning to tell, and even

with his greater strength, they could feel him slowly, slowly losing resources to his weaker opponents. There was something familiar about this enemy, something Mr. Slippery was sure he could see, given time.

Abruptly the enemy pulled away. For a long moment, they held each other's sole attention, like cats waiting for the smallest sign of weakness to launch back into combat—only here the new attack could come from any of ten thousand different directions, from any of the communications nodes that formed their bodies and their minds.

From beside him, he felt Erythrina move forward, as though to lock the other in her green-eyed gaze. "You know who we have here, Slip?" He could tell that all her concentration was on this enemy, that she almost vibrated with the effort. "This is our old friend DON.MAC grown up to super size, and doing his best to disguise himself."

The other seemed to tense and move even further in upon himself. But after a moment, he began imaging. There stood DON.MAC, his face and Plessey-Mercedes body the same as ever. DON.MAC, the first of the Mailman's converts, the one Erythrina was sure had been killed and replaced with a simulator. "And all the time he's been the Mailman. The last person we would suspect, the Mailman's first victim."

DON rolled forward half a meter, his motors keening, his hydraulic fists raised. But he did not deny what Mr. Slippery said. After a moment he seemed to relax. "You are very . . . clever. But then, you two have had help; I never thought you and the cops would cooperate. That was the one combination that had any chance against the 'Mailman.' " He smiled, a familiar automatic twitch. "But don't you see? It's a combination with lethal genes. We three have much more in common than you and the government.

"Look around you. If we were warlocks before, we are gods now. Look!" Without letting the center of their attention wander, the two followed his gaze. As before, the myriad aspects of the lives of billions spread out before them. But now, many things were changed. In their struggle, the three had usurped virtually all of the connected processing power of the human race. Video and phone communications were frozen. The public data bases had lasted long enough to notice that something had gone terribly, terribly wrong. Their last headlines, generated a second before the climax of the battle, were huge banners announcing GREATEST DATA OUTAGE OF ALL TIME. Nearly a billion people watched blank data sets, feeling more panicked than any simple power blackout could ever make them. Already the accumulation of lost data and work time would cause a major recession.

"They are lucky the old arms race is over, or else independent military units would probably have already started a war. Even if we hand back control this instant, it would take them more than a year to get their affairs in order." DON.MAC smirked, the same expression they had seen the day before when he was bragging to the Limey. "There have been few deaths yet. Hospitals and aircraft have some standalone capability."

Even so . . . Mr. Slippery could see thousands of aircraft stacked up over major airports from London to Christchurch. Local computing could never coordinate the safe landing of them all before some ran out of fuel.

"*We* caused all that—with just the fallout of our battle," continued DON. "If we chose to do them harm, I have no doubt we could exterminate the human race." He detonated three warheads in their silos in Utah just to emphasize his point. With dozens of video eyes, in orbit and on the ground, Mr. Slippery and Erythrina watched the destruction sweep across the launch sites. "Consider: how are we different from the gods of myth? And like the gods of myth, we can rule and prosper, just so long as we don't fight among ourselves." He looked expectantly from Mr. Slippery to Erythrina. There was a frown on the Red One's dark face; she seemed to be concentrating on their opponent just as fiercely as ever.

DON.MAC turned back to Mr. Slippery. "Slip, you especially should see that we have no choice but to cooperate. *They know your True Name*. Of the three of us, your life is the most fragile, depending on protecting your body from a government that now considers you a traitor. You would have died a dozen times over during the last thousand seconds if you hadn't used your new powers.

"And you can't go back. Even if you play Boy Scout, destroy me, and return all obedient—even then they will kill you. They know how dangerous you are, perhaps even more dangerous than I. They can't afford to let you exist."

And megalomania aside, that made perfect and chilling sense. As they were talking, a fraction of Mr. Slippery's attention was devoted to confusing and

Vernor Vinge

obstructing the small infantry group that had been air-dropped into the Arcata region just before the government lost all control. Their superiors had realized how easily he could countermand their orders, and so the troops were instructed to ignore all outside direction until they had destroyed a certain Roger Pollack. Fortunately they were depending on city directories and orbit-fed street maps, and he had been keeping them going in circles for some time now. It was a nuisance, and sooner or later he would have to decide on a more permanent solution.

But what was a simple nuisance in his present state would be near-instant death if he returned to his normal self. He looked at Erythrina. Was there any way around DON's arguments?

Her eyes were almost shut, and the frown had deepened. He sensed that more and more of her resources were involved in some pattern analysis. He wondered if she had even heard what DON.MAC said. But after a moment her eyes came open, and she looked at the two of them. There was triumph in that look. "You know, Slip, I don't think I have ever been fooled by a personality simulator, at least not for more than a few minutes."

Mr. Slippery nodded, puzzled by this sudden change in topic. "Sure. If you talk to a simulator long enough, you eventually begin to notice little inflexibilities. I don't think we'll ever be able to write a program that could pass the Turing test."

"Yes, little inflexibilities, a certain lack of imagination. It always seems to be the tipoff. Of course DON here has always pretended to be a program, so it was hard to tell. But I was sure that for the last few months there has been no living being behind his mask . . .

"*. . . and furthermore, I don't think there is anybody there even now.*" Mr. Slippery's attention snapped back to DON.MAC. The other smirked at the accusation. Somehow it was not the right reaction. Mr. Slippery remembered the strange, artificial flavor of DON's combat style. In this short an encounter, there could be no really hard evidence for her theory. She was using her intuition and whatever deep analysis she had been doing these last few seconds.

"But that means we still haven't found the Mailman."

"Right. This is just his best tool. I'll bet the Mailman simply used the pattern he stole from the murdered DON.MAC as the basis for this automatic defense system we've been fighting. The Mailman's time lag is a very real thing, not a red herring at all. Somehow it is the whole secret of who he really is.

"In any case, it makes our present situation a lot easier." She smiled at DON.MAC as though he were a real person. Usually it was easier to behave that way toward simulators; in this case, there was a good deal of triumph in her smile. "You almost won for your master, DON. You almost had us convinced. But now that we know what we are dealing with, it will be easy to—"

Her image flicked out of existence, and Mr. Slippery felt DON grab for the resources Ery controlled. All through near-Earth space, they fought for the weapon systems she had held till an instant before.

And alone, Mr. Slippery could not win. Slowly, slowly, he felt himself bending before the other's force, like some wrestler whose bones were breaking one by one under a murderous opponent. It was all he could do to prevent the DON construct from blasting his home; and to do that, he had to give up progressively more computing power.

Erythrina was gone, gone as though she had never been. Or was she? He gave a sliver of his attention to a search, a sliver that was still many times more powerful than any mere warlock. That tiny piece of consciousness quickly noticed a power failure in southern Rhode Island. Many power failures had developed during the last few minutes, consequent to the data failure. But this one was strange. In addition to power, comm lines were down and even his intervention could not bring them to life. It was about as thoroughly blacked out as a place could be. This could scarcely be an accident.

. . . and there was a voice, barely telephone quality and almost lost in the mass of other data he was processing. *Erythrina!* She had, via some incredibly tortuous detour, retained a communication path to the outside.

His gaze swept the blacked-out Providence suburb. It consisted of new urbapts, perhaps one hundred thousand units in all. Somewhere in there lived the human that was Erythrina. While she had been concentrating on DON.MAC, he must have been working equally hard to find her True Name. Even now, DON did not know precisely who she was, only enough to black out the area she lived in.

It was getting hard to think; DON.MAC was systematically dismantling him. The lethal intent was clear: as soon as Mr. Slippery was sufficiently reduced, the Orbital Lasers would be turned on his body, and then on Erythrina's. And then the Mailman's faithful servant would have a planetary kingdom to turn over to his mysterious master.

He listened to the tiny voice that still leaked out of Providence. It didn't make too much sense. She sounded hysterical, panicked. He was surprised that she could speak at all; she had just suffered—in losing all her computer connections—something roughly analogous to a massive stroke. To her, the world was now seen through a keyhole, incomplete, unknown and dark.

"There is a chance; we still have a chance," the voice went on, hurried and slurred. "An old military communication tower north of here. Damn. I don't know the number or grid, but I can see it from where I'm sitting. With it you could punch through to the roof antenna . . . has plenty of bandwidth, and I've got some battery power here . . . but *hurry*."

She didn't have to tell him that; he was the guy who was being eaten alive. He was almost immobilized now, the other's attack squeezing and stifling where it could not cut and tear. He spasmed against DON's strength and briefly contacted the comm towers north of Providence. Only one of them was in line of sight with the blacked-out area. Its steerable antenna was very, very narrow beam.

"Ery, I'm going to need your house number, maybe even your antenna id."

A second passed, two—a hellish eon for Mr. Slippery. In effect, he had asked her for her True Name—he who was already known to the Feds. Once he returned to the real world, there would be no way he could mask this information from them. He could imagine her thoughts: never again to be free. In her place, he would have paused too, but—

"*Ery!* It's the True Death for both of us if you don't. He's got me!"

This time she barely hesitated. "D-Debby Charteris, 4448 Grosvenor Row. Cut off like this, I don't know the antenna id. Is my name and house enough?"

"Yes. Get ready!"

Even before he spoke, he had already matched the name with an antenna rental and aligned the military antenna on it. Return contact came as he turned his attention back to DON.MAC. With luck, the enemy was not aware of their conversation. Now he must be distracted.

Mr. Slippery surged against the other, breaking communications nodes that served them both. DON shuddered, reorganizing around the resources that were left, then moved in on Mr. Slippery again. Since DON had greater strength to begin with, the maneuver had cost Mr. Slippery proportionately more. The enemy had been momentarily thrown off balance, but now the end would come very quickly.

The spaces around him, once so rich with detail and colors beyond color, were fading now, replaced by the sensations of his true body straining with animal fear in its little house in California. Contact with the greater world was almost gone. He was scarcely aware of it when DON turned the Finger of God back upon him—

Consciousness, the superhuman consciousness of before, returned almost unsensed, unrecognized till awareness brought surprise. Like a strangling victim back from oblivion, Mr. Slippery looked around dazedly, not quite realizing that the struggle continued.

But now the roles were reversed. DON.MAC had been caught by surprise, in the act of finishing off what he thought was his only remaining enemy. Erythrina had used that surprise to good advantage, coming in upon her opponent from a Japanese data center, destroying much of Don's higher reasoning centers before the other was even aware of her. Large, unclaimed processing units lay all about, and as DON and Erythrina continued their struggle, Mr. Slippery quietly absorbed everything in reach.

Even now, DON could have won against either one of them alone, but when Mr. Slippery threw himself back into the battle, they had the advantage. DON.-MAC sensed this too, and with a brazenness that was either mindless or genius, returned to his original appeal. "There is still time! The Mailman will still forgive you."

Mr. Slippery and Erythrina ripped at their enemy from both sides, disconnecting vast blocks of communications, processing and data resources. They denied the Mass Transmits to him, and one by one put the low-level satellites out of synch with his data accesses. DON was confined to land lines, tied into a single military net that stretched from Washington to Denver. He was flailing, randomly using whatever instruments of destruction were still available. All across the midsection of the US, silo missiles detonated, ABM lasers swept back and forth across the sky. The world had been stopped short by the beginning of their struggle, but the ending could tear it to pieces.

The damage to Mr. Slippery and Erythrina was slight, the risk that the random strokes would seriously damage them small. They ignored occasional slashing losses and concentrated single-mindedly on dismantling DON.MAC. They discovered the object code for the simulator that was DON, and zeroed it. DON—or his creator—was clever and had planted many copies, and a new one awakened every time they destroyed the running copy. But as the minutes passed, the simulator found itself with less and less to work with. Now it was barely more than it had been back in the Coven.

"*Fools!* The Mailman is your natural ally. The Feds will *kill* you! Don't you underst—"

The voice stopped in midshriek, as Erythrina zeroed the currently running simulator. No other took up the task. There was a silence, an . . . absence . . . throughout. Erythrina glanced at Mr. Slippery, and the two continued their search through the enemy's territory. This data space was big, and there could be many more copies of DON hidden in it. But without the resources they presently held, the simulator could have no power. It was clear to both of them that no effective ambush could be hidden in these unmoving ruins.

And they had complete copies of DON.MAC to study. It was easy to trace the exact extent of his infection of the system. The two moved systematically, changing what they found so that it would behave as its original programmers had intended. Their work was so thorough that the Feds might never realize just how extensively the Mailman and his henchman had infiltrated them, just how close he had come to total control.

Most of the areas they searched were only slightly

altered and required only small changes. But deep within the military net, there were hundreds of trillions of bytes of program that seemed to have no intelligible function yet were clearly connected with DON's activities. It was apparently object code, but it was so huge and so ill organized that even they couldn't decide if it was more than hash now. There was no possibility that it had any legitimate function; after a few moments' consideration, they randomized it.

At last it was over. Mr. Slippery and Erythrina stood alone. They controlled all connected processing facilities in near-Earth space. There was no place within that volume that any further enemies could be lurking. And there was no evidence that there had ever been interference from beyond.

It was the first time since they had reached this level that they had been able to survey the world without fear. (He scarcely noticed the continuing, pitiful attempts of the American military to kill his real body.) Mr. Slippery looked around him, using all his millions of perceptors. The Earth floated serene. Viewed in the visible, it looked like a thousand pictures he had seen as a human. But in the ultraviolet, he could follow its hydrogen aura out many thousands of kilometers. And the high-energy detectors on satellites at all levels perceived the radiation belts in thousands of energy levels, oscillating in the solar wind. Across the oceans of the world, he could feel the warmth of the currents, see just how fast they were moving. And all the while, he monitored the millions of tiny voices that were now coming back to life as he and Erythrina carefully set the human

race's communication system back on its feet and gently prodded it into function. Every ship in the seas, every aircraft now making for safe landing, every one of the loans, the payments, the meals of an entire race registered clearly on some part of his consciousness. With perception came power; almost everything he saw, he could alter, destroy, or enhance. By the analogical rules of the covens, there was only one valid word for themselves in their present state: they were gods.

". . . we could rule," Erythrina's voice was hushed, self-frightened. "It might be tricky at first, assuring our bodies protection, but we could rule."

"There's still the Mailman—"

She seemed to wave a hand, dismissingly. "Maybe, maybe not. It's true we still are no closer to knowing who he is, but we do know that we have destroyed all his processing power. We would have plenty of warning if he ever tries to reinsinuate himself into the System." She stared at him intently, and it wasn't until some time later that he recognized the faint clues in her behavior and realized that she was holding something back.

What she said was all so clearly true; for as long as their bodies lived, they could rule. And what DON.-MAC had said also seemed true: they were the greatest threat the "forces of law and order" had ever faced, and that included the Mailman. How could the Feds afford to let them be free, how could they even afford to let them *live*, if the two of them gave up the power they had now? But—"A lot of people would have to die if we took over. There are enough independent military entities left on Earth that we'd have to use a good deal of nuclear blackmail, at least at first."

"Yeah," her voice was even smaller than before, and the image of her face was downcast. "During the last few seconds I've done some simulating on that. We'd have to take out four, maybe six, major cities. If there are any command centers hidden from us, it could be a lot worse than that. And we'd have to develop our own human secret-police forces as folks began to operate outside our system. . . . Damn. We'd end up being worse than the human-based government."

She saw the same conclusion in his face and grinned lopsidedly. "You can't do it and neither can I. So the State wins again."

He nodded, "reached" out to touch her briefly. They took one last glorious minute to soak in the higher reality. Then, silently, they parted, each to seek his own way downward.

It was not an instantaneous descent to ordinary humanity. Mr. Slippery was careful to prepare a safe exit. He created a complex set of misdirections for the army unit that was trying to close in on his physical body; it would take them several hours to find him, far longer than necessary for the government to call them off. He set up preliminary negotiations with the Federal programs that had been doing their best to knock him out of power, telling them of his determination to surrender if granted safe passage and safety for his body. In a matter of seconds he would be talking to humans again, perhaps even Virginia, but by then a lot of the basic ground rules would be automatically in operation.

As per their temporary agreements, he closed off first one and then another of the capabilities that he had so recently acquired. It was like stopping one's ears, then blinding one's eyes, but somehow much worse since his very ability to think was being deliberately given up. He was like some lobotomy patient (victim) who only vaguely realizes now what he has lost. Behind him the Federal forces were doing their best to close off the areas he had left, to protect themselves from any change of heart he might have.

Far away now, he could sense Erythrina going through a similar procedure, but more slowly. That was strange; he couldn't be sure with his present faculties, but somehow it seemed that she was deliberately lagging behind and doing something more complicated than was strictly necessary to return safely to normal humanity. And then he remembered that strange look she had given him while saying that they had not figured out who the Mailman was.

One could rule as easily as two!

The panic was sudden and overwhelming, all the more terrible for the feeling of being betrayed by one so trusted. He struck out against the barriers he had so recently allowed to close in about him, but it was too late. He was already weaker than the Feds. Mr. Slippery looked helplessly back into the gathering dimness, and saw . . .

. . . Ery coming down toward the real world with him, giving up the advantage she had held all alone. Whatever problems had slowed her must have had nothing to do with treachery. And somehow his feeling of relief went beyond the mere fact of death avoided—Ery was still what he had always thought her.

* * *

He was seeing a lot of Virginia lately, though of course not socially. Her crew had set up offices in Arcata, and twice a week she and one of her goons would come up to the house. No doubt it was one of the few government operations carried out face-to-face. She or her superiors seemed to realize that anything done over the phone might be subject to trickery. (Which was true, of course. Given several weeks to himself, Pollack could have put together a robot phone connection and—using false ids and priority permits—been on a plane to Djakarta.)

There were a lot of superficial similarities between these meetings and that first encounter the previous spring:

Pollack stepped to the door and watched the black Lincoln pulling up the drive. As always, the vehicle came right into the carport. As always, the driver got out quickly, eyes flickering coldly across Pollack. As always, Virginia moved with military precision (in fact, he had discovered, she had been promoted out of the Army to her present job in DoW intelligence). The two walked purposefully toward the bungalow, ignoring the summer sunlight and the deep wet green of the lawn and pines. He held the door open for them, and they entered with silent arrogance. As always.

He smiled to himself. In one sense nothing had changed. They still had the power of life and death over him. They could still cut him off from everything he loved. But in another sense . . .

"Got an easy one for you today, Pollack," she said as she put her briefcase on the coffee table and enabled its data set. "But I don't think you're going to like it."

"Oh?" He sat down and watched her expectantly.

"The last couple of months, we've had you destroying what remains of the Mailman and getting the National program and data bases back in operation."

Behind everything, there still stood the threat of the Mailman. Ten weeks after the battle—the War, as Virginia called it—the public didn't know any more than that there had been a massive vandalism of the System. Like most major wars, this had left ruination in everyone's camp. The US government and the economy of the entire world had slid far toward chaos in the months after that battle. (In fact, without his work and Erythrina's, he doubted if the US bureaucracies could have survived the Mailman War. He didn't know whether this made them the saviors or the betrayers of America.) But what of the enemy? His power was almost certainly destroyed. In the last three weeks Mr. Slippery had found only one copy of the program kernel that had been DON.MAC, and that had been in nonexecutable form. But the man—or the beings—behind the Mailman was just as anonymous as ever. In that, Virginia, the government, and Pollack were just as ignorant as the general public.

"Now," Virginia continued, "we've got some smaller problems—mopping-up action, you might call it. For nearly two decades, we've had to live with the tuppin vandalism of irresponsible individuals who put their petty self-interest ahead of the public's. Now that we've got you, we intend to put a stop to that:

"We want the True Names of all abusers currently on the System, in particular the members of this so-called coven you used to be a part of."

He had known that the demand would eventually

come, but the knowledge made this moment no less unpleasant. "I'm sorry, I can't."

"Can't? Or won't? See here, Pollack, the price of your freedom is that you play things our way. You've broken enough laws to justify putting you away forever. And we both know that you are so dangerous that you *ought* to be put away. There are people who feel even more strongly than that, Pollack, people who are not as soft in the head as I am. They simply want you and your girl friend in Providence safely dead." The speech was delivered with characteristic flat bluntness, but she didn't quite meet his eyes as she spoke. Ever since he had returned from the battle, there had been a faint diffidence behind her bluster.

She covered it well, but it was clear to Pollack that she didn't know if she should fear him or respect him—or both. In any case, she seemed to recognize a basic mystery in him; she had more imagination than he had originally thought. It was a bit amusing, for there was very little special about Roger Pollack, the man. He went from day to day feeling a husk of what he had once been and trying to imagine what he could barely remember.

Roger smiled almost sympathetically. "I can't *and* I won't, Virginia. And I don't think you will harm me for it—Let me finish. The only thing that frightens your bosses more than Erythrina and me is the possibility that there may be other unknown persons—maybe even the Mailman, back from wherever he has disappeared to—who might be equally powerful. She and I are your only real experts on this type of subversion. I bet that even if they could, your people wouldn't train their own clean-cut, braided types as replacements for us. The more paranoid a security organization is, the less likely it is to trust anyone with this sort of power. Mr. Slippery and Erythrina are the known factors, the experts who turned back from the brink. Our restraint was the only thing that stood between the Powers That Be and the Powers That Would Be."

Virginia was speechless for a moment, and Pollack could see that this was the crux of her changed attitude toward him. All her life she had been taught that the individual is corrupted by power: she boggled at the notion that he had been offered mastery of all mankind—and had refused it.

Finally she smiled, a quick smile that was gone almost before he noticed it. "Okay. I'll pass on what you say. You may be right. The vandals are a long-range threat to our basic American freedoms, but day to day, they are a mere annoyance. My superiors—the Department of Welfare—are probably willing to fight them as we have in the past. They'll tolerate your, uh, disobedience *in this single matter* as long as you and Erythrina loyally protect us against the superhuman threats."

Pollack felt a great sense of relief. He had been so afraid DoW would be willing to destroy him for this refusal. And since the Feds would never be free of their fear of the Mailman, he and Debby Charteris—Erythrina—would never be forced to betray their friends.

"But," continued the cop, "that doesn't mean you get to ignore the covens. The most likely place for superhuman threats to resurface is from within them. The vandals are the people with the most real experience on the System—even the Army is beginning to see that. And if a superhuman type originates outside the covens, we figure his ego will still make him show off to them, just as with the Mailman.

"In addition to your other jobs, we want you to spend a couple of hours a week with each of the major covens. You'll be one of the 'boys'—only now you're under responsible control, watching for any sign of Mailman-type influence."

"I'll get to see Ery again!"

"No. That rule still stands. And you should be grateful. I don't think we could tolerate your existence if there weren't two of you. With only one in the Other Plane at a time, we'll always have a weapon in reserve. And as long as we can keep you from meeting there, we can keep you from scheming against us. This is serious, Roger: if we catch you two or your surrogates playing around in the Other Plane, it will be the end."

"Hmm."

She looked hard at him for a moment, then appeared to take that for acquiescence. The next half-hour was devoted to the details of this week's assignments. (It would have been easier to feed him all this when he was in the Other Plane, but Virginia—or at least DoW—seemed wedded to the past.) He was to continue the work on Social Security Records and the surveillance of the South American data nets. There was an enormous amount of work to be done, at least with the limited powers the Feds were willing to give him. It would likely be October before the welfare machinery was working properly again. But that would be in time for the elections.

Then, late in the week, they wanted him to visit the Coven. Roger knew he would count the hours; it had been so long.

Virginia was her usual self, intense and all business, until she and her driver were ready to leave. Standing in the carport, she said almost shyly, "I ran your *Anne Boleyn* last week . . . It's really very good."

"You sound surprised."

"No. I mean yes, maybe I was. Actually I've run it several times, usually with the viewpoint character set to Anne. There seems to be a lot more depth to it than other participation games I've read. I've got the feeling that if I am clever enough, someday I'll stop Henry and keep my head!"

Pollack grinned. He could imagine Virginia, the hard-eyed cop, reading *Anne* to study the psychology of her client-prisoner—then gradually getting caught up in the action of the novel. "It is possible."

In fact, it was possible she might turn into a rather nice human being someday.

But by the time Pollack was starting back up the walk to his house, Virginia was no longer on his mind. He was going back to the Coven!

A chill mist that was almost rain blew across the hillside and obscured the far distance in shifting patches. But even from here, on the ridge above the swamp, the castle looked different: heavier, stronger, darker.

Mr. Slippery started down the familiar slope. The frog on his shoulder seemed to sense his unease and its clawlets bit tighter into the leather of his jacket. Its beady yellow eyes turned this way and that, re-

cording everything. (Altogether, that frog was much improved—almost out of amateur status nowadays.)

The traps were different. In just the ten weeks since the War, the Coven had changed them more than in the previous two years. Every so often, he shook the gathering droplets of water from his face and peered more closely at a bush or boulder by the side of the path. His advance was slow, circuitous, and interrupted by invocations of voice and hand.

Finally he stood before the towers. A figure of black and glowing red climbed out of the magma moat to meet him. Even Alan had changed: he no longer had his asbestos T-shirt, and there was no humor in his sparring with the visitor. Mr. Slippery had to stare upward to look directly at his massive head. The elemental splashed molten rock down on them, and the frog scampered between his neck and collar, its skin cold and slimy against his own. The passwords were different, the questioning more hostile, but Mr. Slippery was a match for the tests and in a matter of minutes Alan retreated sullenly to his steaming pool, and the drawbridge was lowered for their entrance.

The hall was almost the same as before: perhaps a bit drier, more brightly lit. There were certainly more people. And they were all looking at him as he stood in the entranceway. Mr. Slippery gave his traveling jacket and hat to a liveried servant and started down the steps, trying to recognize the faces, trying to understand the tension and hostility that hung in the air.

"Slimey!" The Limey stepped forward from the crowd, a familiar grin splitting his bearded face.

"Slip! Is that really you?" (Not entirely a rhetorical question, under the circumstances.)

Mr. Slippery nodded, and after a moment, the other did, too. The Limey almost ran across the space that separated them, stuck out his hand, and clapped the other on the shoulder. "Come on, come on! We have rather a lot to talk about!"

As if on cue, the others turned back to their conversations and ignored the two friends as they walked to one of the sitting rooms that opened off the main hall. Mr. Slippery felt like a man returning to his old school ten years after graduation. Almost all the faces were different, and he had the feeling that he could never belong here again. But this was only ten weeks, not ten years.

The Slimey Limey shut the heavy door, and the sounds from the main room were muted. He waved Slip to a chair and made a show of mixing them some drinks.

"They're all simulators, aren't they?" Slip said quietly.

"Uh?" The Limey broke off his stream of chatter and shook his head glumly. "Not all. I've recruited four or five apprentices. They do their best to make the place look thriving and occupied. You may have noticed various improvements in our security."

"It looks stronger, but it's more appearance than fact."

Slimey shrugged. "I really didn't expect it to fool the likes of you."

Mr. Slippery leaned forward. "Who's left from the old group, Slimey?"

"DON's gone. The Mailman is gone. Wiley J. Bastard shows up a couple of times a month, but he's not much fun anymore. I think Erythrina's still on the System, but she hasn't come by. I thought you were gone until today."

"What about Robin Hood?"

"Gone."

That accounted for all the top talents. Virginia the Frog hadn't been giving away all that much when she excused him from betraying the Coven. Slip wondered if there was any hint of smugness in the frog's fixed and lipless smile.

"What happened?"

The other sighed. "There's a depression on down in the real world, in case you hadn't noticed; and it's being blamed on us vandals.

"—I know, that could scarcely explain Robin's disappearance, only the lesser ones. Slip, I think most of our old friends are either dead—Truly Dead—or very frightened that if they come back into this Plane, they will become Truly Dead."

This felt very much like history repeating itself. "How do you mean?"

The Limey leaned forward. "Slip, it's quite obvious the government's feeding us lies about what caused the depression. They say it was a combination of programming errors and the work of 'vandals.' We know that can't be true. No ordinary vandals could cause that sort of damage. Right after the crash, I looked at what was left of the Feds' data bases. Whatever ripped things up was more powerful than any vandal. . . . And I've spoken with—p'raps I should say interrogated—Wiley. I think what we see in the real world and on this plane is in fact the wreckage of a bloody major war."

Vernor Vinge

"Between?"

"Creatures as far above me as I am above a chimp. The names we know them by are the Mailman, Erythrina . . . and just possibly Mr. Slippery."

"Me?" Slip tensed and sent out probes along the communications links which he perceived had created the image before him. Even though on a leash, Mr. Slippery was far more powerful than any normal warlock, and it should have been easy to measure the power of this potential opponent. But the Limey was a diffuse, almost nebulous presence. Slip couldn't tell if he were facing an opponent in the same class as himself; in fact, he had no clear idea of the other's strength, which was even more ominous.

The Limey didn't seem to notice. "That's what I thought. Now I doubt it. I wager you were used—like Wiley and possibly DON—by the other combatants. And I see that now you're in *someone's* thrall." His finger stabbed at the yellow-eyed frog on Mr. Slippery's shoulder, and a sparkle of whiskey flew into the creature's face. Virginia—or whoever was controlling the beast—didn't know what to do, and the frog froze momentarily, then recovered its wits and emitted a pale burst of flame.

The Limey laughed. "But it's no one very competent. The Feds is my guess. What happened? Did they sight your True Name, or did you just sell out?"

"The creature's my familiar, Slimey. We all have our apprentices. If you really believe we're the Feds, why did you let us in?"

The other shrugged. "Because there are enemies and enemies, Slip. Beforetime, we called the government the Great Enemy. Now I'd say they are just one in a pantheon of nasties. Those of us who survived the crash are a lot tougher, a lot less frivolous. We don't think of this as all a wry game anymore. And we're teaching our apprentices a lot more systematically. It's not near so much fun. Now when we talk of traitors in the Coven, we mean real, life-and-death treachery.

"But it's necessary. When it comes to it, if we little people don't protect ourselves, we're going to be eaten up by the government or . . . certain other creatures I fear even more."

The frog shifted restively on Mr. Slippery's shoulder, and he could imagine Virginia getting ready to deliver some speech on the virtue of obeying the laws of society in order to reap its protection. He reached across to pat its cold and pimply back; now was not the time for such debate.

"You had one of the straightest heads around here, Slip. Even if you aren't one of us anymore, I don't reckon you're an absolute enemy. You and your . . . friend may have certain interests in common with us. There are things you should know about—if you don't already. An' p'raps there'll be times you'll help us similarly."

Slip felt the Federal tether loosen. Virginia must have convinced her superiors that there was actually help to be had here. "Okay. You're right. There was a war. The Mailman was the enemy. He lost and now we're trying to put things back together."

"Ah, that's just it, old man. *I don't think the war is over*. True, all that remains of the Mailman's constructs are 'craterfields' spread through the government's program space. But something like him is still very much alive." He saw the disbelief in Mr. Slippery's face. "I know, you an' your friends are more powerful than any of us. But there are many of us—not just in the Coven—and we have learned a lot these past ten weeks. There are signs, so light an' fickle you might call 'em atmosphere, that tell us something like the Mailman is still alive. It doesn't quite have the texture of the Mailman, but it's there."

Mr. Slippery nodded. He didn't need any special explanations of the feeling. *Damn! If I weren't on a leash, I would have seen all this weeks ago, instead of finding it out secondhand.* He thought back to those last minutes of their descent from godhood and felt a chill. He knew what he must ask now, and he had a bad feeling about what the answer might be. Somehow he had to prevent Virginia from hearing that answer. It would be a great risk, but he still had a few tricks he didn't think DoW knew of. He probed back along the links that went to Arcata and D.C., feeling the interconnections and the redundancy checks. If he was lucky, he would not have to alter more than a few hundred bits of the information that would flow down to them in the next few seconds. "So who do you think is behind it?"

"For a while, I thought it might be you. Now I've seen you and, uh, done some tests, I know you're more powerful than in the old days and probably more powerful than I am now, but you're no superman."

"Maybe I'm in disguise."

"Maybe, but I doubt it." The Limey was coming closer to the critical words that must be disguised. Slip began to alter the redundancy bits transmitted through the construct of the frog. He would have to fake the record both before and after those words if the deception was to escape detection completely. "No, there's a certain style to this presence. A style that reminds me of our old friend, REorbyitnh rHionoad." The name he said, and the name Mr. Slippery heard, was "Erythrina." The name blended imperceptibly in its place, the name the frog heard, and reported, was "Robin Hood."

"Hmm, possible. He always seemed to be power hungry." The Limey's eyebrows went up fractionally at the pronoun "he." Besides, Robin had been a fantastically clever vandal, not a power grabber. Slimey's eyes flickered toward the frog, and Mr. Slippery prayed that he would play along. "Do you really think this is as great a threat as the Mailman?"

"Who knows? The presence isn't as widespread as the Mailman's, and since the crash no more of us have disappeared. Also, I'm not sure that . . . he . . . is the only such creature left. Perhaps the original Mailman is still around."

And you can't decide who it is that I'm really trying to fool, can you?

The discussion continued for another half-hour, a weird three-way fencing match with just two active players. On the one hand, he and the Limey were trying to communicate past the frog, and on the other, the Slimey Limey was trying to decide if perhaps Slip was the real enemy and the frog a potential ally. The hell of it was, Mr. Slippery wasn't sure himself of the answer to that puzzle.

Slimey walked him out to the drawbridge. For a few moments, they stood on the graven ceramic plating and spoke. Below them, Alan paddled back and forth, looking up at them uneasily. The mist was a light rain now, and a constant sizzling came from the molten rock.

Finally Slip said, "You're right in a way, Slimey. I am someone's thrall. But I will look for Robin Hood. If you're right, you've got a couple of new allies. If he's too strong for us, this might be the last you see of me."

The Slimey Limey nodded, and Slip hoped he had gotten the real message: He would take on Ery all by himself.

"Well then, let's hope this ain't good-bye, old man."

Slip walked back down into the valley, aware of the Limey's not unsympathetic gaze on his back.

How to find her, how to speak with her? And survive the experience, that is. Virginia had forbidden him—literally on pain of death—from meeting with Ery on this plane. Even if he could do so, it would be a deadly risk for other reasons. What had Ery been doing in those minutes she dallied, when she had fooled him into descending back to the human plane before her? At the time, he had feared it was a betrayal. Yet he had lived and had forgotten the mystery. Now he wondered again. It was impossible for him to understand the complexity of those minutes. Perhaps she had weakened herself at the beginning to gull him into starting the descent, and perhaps then she hadn't been quite strong enough to take over. Was that possible? And now she was slowly, secretly building back her powers, just as the Mailman had done? He didn't want to believe it, and he knew if Virginia heard his suspicions, the Feds would kill her immediately. There would be no trial, no deep investigation.

Somehow he must get past Virginia and confront Ery—confront her in such a way that he could destroy her if she were a new Mailman. *And there is a way!* He almost laughed: it was absurd and absurdly simply, and it was the only thing that might work. All eyes were on this plane, where magic and power flowed easily to the participants. He would attack from beneath, from the lowly magicless real world!

But there was one final act of magic he must slip past Virginia, something absolutely necessary for a real world confrontation with Erythrina.

He had reached the far ridge and was starting down the hillside that led to the swamps. Even preoccupied, he had given the right signs flawlessly. The guardian sprites were not nearly so vigilant toward contructs moving away from the castle. As the wet brush closed in about them, the familiar red and black spider—or its cousin—swung down from above.

"Beware, beware," came the tiny voice. From the flecks of gold across its abdomen, he knew the right response: left hand up and flick the spider away. Instead Slip raised his right hand and struck at the creature.

The spider hoisted itself upward, screeching faintly, then dropped toward Slip's neck—to land squarely on the frog. A free-for-all erupted as the two scrambled across the back of his neck, pale flame jousting against venom. Even as he moved to save the frog, Mr. Slippery melted part of his attention into a data line that fed a sporting goods store in Montreal. An order was placed and later that day a certain very special pack-

TRUE NAMES

age would be in the mail to the Boston International Rail Terminal.

Slip made a great show of dispatching the spider, and as the frog settled back on his shoulder, he saw that he had probably fooled Virginia. That he had expected. Fooling Ery would be much the deadlier, chancier thing.

If this afternoon were typical, then July in Providence must be a close approximation to Hell. Roger Pollack left the tube as it passed the urbapt block and had to walk nearly four hundred meters to get to the tower he sought. His shirt was soaked with sweat from just below the belt line right up to his neck. The contents of the package he had picked up at the airport train station sat heavily in his right coat pocket, tapping against his hip with every step, reminding him that this was high noon in more ways than one.

Pollack quickly crossed the blazing concrete plaza and walked along the edge of the shadow that was all the tower cast in the noonday sun. All around him the locals swarmed, all ages, seemingly unfazed by the still, moist, hot air. Apparently you could get used to practically anything.

Even an urbapt in summer in Providence. Pollack had expected the buildings to be more depressing. Workers who had any resources became data commuters and lived outside the cities. Of course, some of the people here were data-set users too and so could be characterized as data commuters. Many of them worked as far away from home as any exurb dweller. The difference was that they made so little money (when they had a job at all) that they were forced to take advantage of the economies of scale the urbapts provided.

Pollack saw the elevator ahead but had to detour around a number of children playing stickball in the plaza. The elevator was only half-full, so a wave from him was all it took to keep it grounded till he could get aboard.

No one followed him on, and the faces around him were disinterested and entirely ordinary. Pollack was not fooled. He hadn't violated the letter of Virginia's law; he wasn't trying to see Erythrina on the data net. But he was going to see Debby Charteris, which came close to being the same thing. He imagined the Feds debating with themselves, finally deciding it would be safe to let the two godlings get together if it were on this plane where the *State* was still the ultimate, all-knowing god. He and Debby would be observed. Even so, he would somehow discover if she were the threat the Limey saw. If not, the Feds would never know of his suspicions. But if Ery had betrayed them all and meant to set herself up in place of—or in league with—the Mailman, then in the next few minutes one of them would die.

The express slid to a stop with a deceptive gentleness that barely gave a feeling of lightness. Pollack paid and got off.

Floor 25 was mainly shopping mall. He would have to find the stairs to the residential apts between Floors 25 and 35. Pollack drifted through the mall. He was beginning to feel better about the whole thing. *I'm still alive, aren't I?* If Ery had really become what the Limey and Slip feared, then he probably would have had a little "accident" before now. All the way across the continent he sat with his guts frozen, thinking how easy it would be for someone with the Mailman's power to destroy an air transport, even without resorting to the military's lasers. A tiny change in navigation or traffic-control directions, and any number of fatal incidents could be arranged. But nothing had happened, which meant that either Ery was innocent or that she hadn't noticed him. (And that second possibility was unlikely if she were a new Mailman. One impression that remained stronger than any other from his short time as godling was the omniscience of it all.)

It turned out the stairs were on the other side of the mall, marked by a battered sign reminiscent of old-time highway markers: FOOTS > 26–30. The place wasn't really too bad, he supposed, eyeing the stained but durable carpet that covered the stairs. And the hallways coming off each landing reminded him of the motels he had known as a child, before the turn of the century. There was very little trash visible, the people moving around him weren't poorly dressed, and there was only the faintest spice of disinfectant in the air. Apt module 28355, where Debbie Charteris lived, might be high-class. It did have an exterior view, he knew that. Maybe Erythrina—Debbie—*liked* living with all these other people. Surely, now that the government was so interested in her, she could move anywhere she wished.

But when he reached it, he found floor 28 no different from the others he had seen: carpeted hallway stretching away forever beneath dim lights that showed identical module doorways dwindling in

TRUE NAMES

perspective. What was Debbie/Erythrina like that she would choose to live here?

"Hold it." Three teenagers stepped from behind the slant of the stairs. Pollack's hand edged toward his coat pocket. He had heard of the gangs. These three looked like heavies, but they were well and conservatively dressed, and the small one actually had his hair in a braid. They wanted very much to be thought part of the establishment.

The short one flashed something silver at him. "Building Police." And Pollack remembered the news stories about Federal Urban Support paying youngsters for urbapt security: "A project that saves money and staff, while at the same time giving our urban youth an opportunity for responsible citizenship."

Pollack swallowed. Best to treat them like real cops. He showed them his id. "I'm from out of state. I'm just visiting."

The other two closed in, and the short one laughed. "That's sure. Fact, Mr. Pollack, Sammy's little gadget says you're in violation of Building Ordinance." The one on Pollack's left waved a faintly buzzing cylinder across Pollack's jacket, then pushed a hand into the jacket and withdrew Pollack's pistol, a lightweight ceramic slug-gun perfect for hunting hikes—and which should have been perfect for getting past a building's weapon detectors.

Sammy smiled down at the weapon, and the short one continued, "Thing you didn't know, Mr. Pollack, is Federal law requires a metal tag in the butt of these cram guns. Makes 'em easy to detect." Until the tag was removed. Pollack suspected that somehow this incident might never be reported.

The three stepped back, leaving the way clear for Pollack. "That's all? I can go?"

The young cop grinned. "Sure. You're out-of-towner. How could you know?"

Pollack continued down the hall. The others did not follow. Pollack was fleetingly surprised: maybe the FUS project actually worked. Before the turn of the century, goons like those three would have at least robbed him. Instead they behaved something like real cops.

Or maybe—and he almost stumbled at this new thought—*they all work for Ery now*. That might be the first symptom of conquest: the new god would simply become the government. And he—the last threat to the new order—was being granted one last audience with the victor.

Pollack straightened and walked on more quickly. There was no turning back now, and he was damned if he would show any more fear. Besides, he thought with a sudden surge of relief, it was out of his control now. If Ery was a monster, there was nothing he could do about it; he would not have to try to kill her. If she were not, then his own survival would be proof, and he need think of no complicated tests of her innocence.

He was almost hurrying now. He had always wanted to know what the human being beyond Erythrina was like; sooner or later he would have had to do this anyway. Weeks ago he had looked through all the official directories for the state of Rhode Island, but there wasn't much to find: Linda and Deborah Charteris lived at 28355 Place on 4448 Grosvenor Row. The public directory didn't even show their "interests and occupations."

28313, 315, 317. . . .

His mind had gone in circles, generating all the things Debby Charteris might turn out to be. She would not be the exotic beauty she projected in the Other Plane. That was too much to hope for; but the other possibilities vied in his mind. He had lived with each, trying to believe that he could accept whatever turned out to be the case:

Most likely, she was a perfectly ordinary looking person who lived in an urbapt to save enough money to buy high-quality processing equipment and rent dense comm lines. Maybe she wasn't good-looking, and that was why the directory listing was relatively secretive.

Almost as likely, she was massively handicapped. He had seen that fairly often among the warlocks whose True Names he knew. They had extra medical welfare and used all their free money for equipment that worked around whatever their problem might be—paraplegia, quadriplegia, multiple sense loss. As such, they were perfectly competitive on the job market, yet old prejudices often kept them out of normal society. Many of these types retreated into the Other Plane, where one could completely control one's appearance.

And then, since the beginning of time, there had been the people who simply did not like reality, who wanted another world, and if given half a chance would live there forever. Pollack suspected that some of the best warlocks might be of this type. Such people were content to live in an urbapt, to spend all their money on processing and life-support equipment, to spend days at a time in the Other Plane, never

TRUE NAMES

moving, never exercising their real world bodies. They grew more and more adept, more and more knowledgeable—while their bodies slowly wasted. Pollack could imagine such a person becoming an evil thing and taking over the Mailman's role. It would be like a spider sitting in its web, its victims all humanity. He remembered Ery's contemptuous attitude on learning he never used drugs to maintain concentration and so stay longer in the Other Plane. He shuddered.

And there, finally, and yet too soon, the numbers 28355 stood on the wall before him, the faint hall light glistening off their bronze finish. For a long moment, he balanced between the fear and the wish. Finally he reached forward and tapped the door buzzer.

Fifteen seconds passed. There was no one nearby in the hall. From the corner of his eye, he could see the "cops" lounging by the stairs. About a hundred meters the other way, an argument was going on. The contenders rounded the faraway corner and their voices quieted, leaving him in near silence.

There was a click, and a small section of the door became transparent, a window (more likely a holo) on the interior of the apt. And the person beyond that view would be either Deborah or Linda Charteris.

"Yes?" The voice was faint, cracking with age. Pollack saw a woman barely tall enough to come up to the pickup on the other side. Her hair was white, visibly thin on top, especially from the angle he was viewing.

"I'm . . . I'm looking for Deborah Charteris."

"My granddaughter. She's out shopping. Downstairs in the mall, I think." The head bobbed, a faintly distracted nod.

TRUE NAMES

"Oh. Can you tell me—" *Deborah, Debby.* It suddenly struck him what an old-fashioned name that was, more the name of a grandmother than a granddaughter. He took a quick step to the door and looked down through the pane so that he could see most of the other's body. The woman wore an old-fashioned skirt and blouse combination of some brilliant red material.

Pollack pushed his hand against the immovable plastic of the door. "Ery, please. Let me in."

The pane blanked as he spoke, but after a moment the door slowly opened. "Okay." Her voice was tired, defeated. Not the voice of a god boasting victory.

The interior was decorated cheaply and with what might have been good taste except for the garish excesses of red on red. Pollack remembered reading somewhere that as you age, color sensitivity decreases. This room might seem only mildly bright to the person Erythrina had turned out to be.

The woman walked slowly across the tiny apt and gestured for him to sit. She was frail, her back curved in a permanent stoop, her every step considered yet tremulous. Under the apt's window, he noticed an elaborate GE processor system. Pollack sat and found himself looking slightly upward into her face.

"Slip—or maybe I should call you Roger here—you always were a bit of a romantic fool." She paused for breath, or perhaps her mind wandered. "I was beginning to think you had more sense than to come out here, that you could leave well enough alone."

"You . . . you mean, you didn't know I was coming?" The knowledge was a great loosening in his chest.

"Not until you were in the building." She turned and sat carefully upon the sofa.

"I had to see who you really are," and that was certainly the truth. "After this spring, there is no one the likes of us in the whole world."

Her face cracked in a little smile. "And now you see how different we are. I had hoped you never would and that someday they would let us back together on the Other Plane. . . . But in the end, it doesn't really matter." She paused, brushed at her temple, and frowned as though forgetting something, or remembering something else.

"I never did look much like the Erythrina you know. I was never tall, of course, and my hair was never red. But I didn't spend my whole life selling life insurance in Peoria, like poor Wiley."

"You . . . you must go all the way back to the beginning of computing."

She smiled again, and nodded just so, a mannerism Pollack had often seen on the Other Plane. "Almost, almost. Out of high school, I was a keypunch operator. You know what a keypunch is?"

He nodded hesitantly, visions of some sort of machine press in his mind.

"It was a dead-end job, and in those days they'd keep you in it forever if you didn't get out under your own power. I got out of it and into college quick as I could, but at least I can say I was in the business during the stone age. After college, I never looked back; there was always so much happening. In the Nasty Nineties, I was on the design of the ABM and FoG control programs. The whole team, the whole of DoD for that matter, was trying to program the thing with procedural languages; it would take 'em a thousand years and a couple of wars to do it that way, and they were beginning to realize as much. I was responsible for getting them away from CRTs, for getting into really interactive EEG programming—what they call portal programming nowadays. Sometimes . . . sometimes when my ego needs a little help, I like to think that if I had never been born, hundreds of millions more would have died back then, and our cities would be glassy ponds today.

". . . And along the way there was a marriage . . ." her voice trailed off again, and she sat smiling at memories Pollack could not see.

He looked around the apt. Except for the processor and a fairly complete kitchenette, there was no special luxury. What money she had must go into her equipment, and perhaps in getting a room with a real exterior view. Beyond the rising towers of the Grosvenor complex, he could see the nest of comm towers that had been their last-second salvation that spring. When he looked back at her, he saw that she was watching him with an intent and faintly amused expression that was very familiar.

"I'll bet you wonder how anyone so daydreamy could be the Erythrina you knew in the Other Plane."

"Why, no," he lied. "You seem perfectly lucid to me."

"Lucid, yes. I am still that, thank God. But I know—and no one has to tell me—that I can't support a train of thought like I could before. These last two or three years, I've found that my mind can wander, can drop into reminiscence, at the most inconvenient times. I've had one stroke, and about all 'the miracles of modern medicine' can do for me is predict that it will not be the last one.

"But in the Other Plane, I can compensate. It's easy for the EEG to detect failure of attention. I've written a package that keeps a thirty-second backup; when distraction is detected, it forces attention and reloads my short-term memory. Most of the time, this gives me better concentration than I've ever had in my life. And when there is a really serious wandering of attention, the package can interpolate for a number of seconds. You may have noticed that, though perhaps you mistook it for poor communications coordination."

She reached a thin, blue-veined hand toward him. He took it in his own. It felt so light and dry, but it returned his squeeze. "It really is me—Ery—inside, Slip."

He nodded, feeling a lump in his throat.

"When I was a kid, there was this song, something about us all being aging children. And it's so very, very true. Inside I still feel like a youngster. But on this plane, no one else can see . . ."

"But I know, Ery. We knew each other on the Other Plane, and I know what you truly are. Both of us are so much more there than we could ever be here." This was all true: even with the restrictions they put on him now, he had a hard time understanding all he did on the Other Plane. What he had become since the spring was a fuzzy dream to him when he was down in the physical world. Sometimes he felt like a fish trying to imagine what a man in an airplane might be feeling. He never spoke of it like this to Virginia and her friends: they would be sure he had finally gone crazy. It was far beyond what he had known as a warlock. And what they had been those brief minutes last spring had been equally far beyond that.

"Yes, I think you do know me, Slip. And we'll be . . . friends as long as this body lasts. And when I'm gone—"

"I'll remember; I'll always remember you, Ery."

She smiled and squeezed his hand again. "Thanks. But that's not what I was getting at. . . ." Her gaze drifted off again. "I figured out who the Mailman was and I wanted to tell you."

Pollack could imagine Virginia and the other DoW eavesdroppers hunkering down to their spy equipment. "I hoped you knew something." He went on to tell her about the Slimey Limey's detection of Mailman-like operations still on the System. He spoke carefully, knowing that he had two audiences.

Ery—even now he couldn't think of her as Debby—nodded. "I've been watching the Coven. They've grown, these last months. I think they take themselves more seriously now. In the old days, they never would have noticed what the Limey warned you about. But it's not the Mailman he saw, Slip."

"How can you be sure, Ery? We never killed more than his service programs and his simulators—like DON.MAC. We never found his True Name. We don't even know if he's human or some science-fictional alien."

"You're wrong, Slip. I know what the Limey saw, and I know who the Mailman is—or was," she spoke quietly, but with certainty. "It turns out the Mailman was the greatest cliché of the Computer Age, maybe of the entire Age of Science."

"Huh?"

"You've seen plenty of personality simulators in the Other Plane. DON.MAC—at least as he was rewritten by the Mailman—was good enough to fool normal warlocks. Even Alan, the Coven's elemental, shows plenty of human emotion and cunning." Pollack thought of the new Alan, so ferocious and intimidating. The Turing T-shirt was beneath his dignity now. "Even so, Slip, I don't think you've ever believed you could be permanently fooled by a simulation, have you?"

"Wait. Are you trying to tell me that the Mailman was just another simulator? That the time lag was just to obscure the fact that he was a simulator? That's ridiculous. You know his powers were more than human, almost as great as ours became."

"But do you think you could ever be fooled?"

"Frankly, no. If you talk to one of those things long enough, they display a repetitiveness, an inflexibility that's a giveaway. I don't know; maybe someday there'll be programs that can pass the Turing test. But whatever it is that makes a person a person is terribly complicated. Simulation is the wrong way to get at it, because being a person is more than symptoms. A program that was a person would use enormous data bases, and if the processors running it were the sort we have now, you certainly couldn't expect real-time interaction with the outside world." And Pollack suddenly had a glimmer of what she was thinking.

"That's the critical point, Slip: *if you want real-time interaction*. But the Mailman—the sentient, conversational part—never did operate real time. We thought the lag was a communications delay that showed the operator was off-planet, but really he was here all the time. It just took him hours of processing time to sustain seconds of self-awareness."

Pollack opened his mouth, but nothing came out. It went against all his intuition, almost against what religion he had, but it might just barely be possible. The Mailman had controlled immense resources. All his quick time reactions could have been the work of ordinary programs and simulators like DON.MAC. The only evidence they had for his humanity were those teleprinter conversations where his responses were spread over hours.

"Okay, for the sake of argument, let's say it's possible. Someone, somewhere had to write the original Mailman. Who was that?"

"Who would you guess? The government, of course. About ten years ago. It was an NSA team trying to automate system protection. Some brilliant people, but they could never really get it off the ground. They wrote a developmental kernel that by itself was not especially effective or aware. It was designed to live within large systems and gradually grow in power and awareness, *independent* of what policies or mistakes the operators of the system might make.

"The program managers saw the Frankenstein analogy—or at least they saw a threat to their personal power—and quashed the project. In any case, it was very expensive. The program executed slowly and gobbled incredible data space."

"And you're saying that someone conveniently left a copy running all unknown?"

She seemed to miss the sarcasm. "It's not that unlikely. Research types are fairly careless—outside of their immediate focus. When I was in FoG, we lost thousands of megabytes 'between the cracks' of our data bases. And back then, that was a lot of memory. The development kernel is not very large. My guess is a copy was left in the system. Remember, the kernel was designed to live untended if it ever started executing. Over the years it slowly grew—both because of its natural tendencies and because of the increased power of the nets it lived in."

Pollack sat back on the sofa. Her voice was tiny and frail, so unlike the warm, rich tones he remembered from the Other Plane. But she spoke with the same authority.

Debby's—Erythrina's—pale eyes stared off beyond the walls of the apt, dreaming. "You know, they are right to be afraid," she said finally. "Their world is ending. Even without us, there would still be the Limey, the Coven—and someday most of the human race."

Damn. Pollack was momentarily tongue-tied, trying desperately to think of something to mollify the threat implicit in Ery's words. *Doesn't she understand that DoW would never let us talk unbugged? Doesn't she know how trigger-happy scared the top Feds must be by now?*

But before he could say anything, Ery glanced at him, saw the consternation in his face, and smiled. The tiny hand patted his. "Don't worry, Slip. The Feds are listening, but what they're hearing is tearful chitchat—you overcome to find me what I am, and me trying to console the both of us. They will never know what I really tell you here. They will never know about the gun the local boys took off you."

"What?"

"You see, I lied a little. I know why you really came. I know you thought that *I* might be the new monster. But I don't want to lie to you anymore. You risked your life to find out the truth, when you could have just told the Feds what you guessed." She went on, taking advantage of his stupefied silence. "Did you ever wonder what I did in those last minutes this spring, after we surrendered—when I lagged behind you in the Other Plane?

"It's true, we really did destroy the Mailman; that's what all that unintelligible data space we plowed up was. I'm sure there are copies of the kernel hidden here and there, like little cancers in the System, but we can control them one by one as they appear.

"I guessed what had happened when I saw all that space, and I had plenty of time to study what was left, even to trace back to the original research project. Poor little Mailman, like the monsters of fiction—he was only doing what he had been designed to do. He was taking over the System, protecting it from everyone—even its owners. I suspect he would have announced himself in the end and used some sort of nuclear blackmail to bring the rest of the world into line. But even though his programs had been running for several years, he had only had fifteen or twenty hours of human type self-awareness when we did him in. His personality programs were that slow. He never attained the level of consciousness you and I had on the System.

"But he really was self-aware, and that was the triumph of it all. And in those few minutes, I figured out how I could adapt the basic kernel to accept any input personality. . . . That is what I really wanted to tell you."

"Then what the Limey saw was—"

She nodded. "Me . . ."

She was grinning now, an open though conspiratorial grin that was very familiar. "When Bertrand Russell was very old, and probably as dotty as I am now, he talked of spreading his interests and attention out to the greater world and away from his own body, so that when that body died he would scarcely notice it, his whole consciousness would be so diluted through the outside world.

"For him, it was wishful thinking, of course. But not for me. My kernel is out there in the System. Every time I'm there, I transfer a little more of myself. The kernel is growing into a true Erythrina, who is also truly me. When this body dies," she squeezed his hand with hers, "when this body dies, *I* will still be, and you can still talk to me."

"Like the Mailman?"

"Slow like the Mailman. At least till I design faster processors. . . .

". . . So in a way, I am everything you and the Limey were afraid of. *You* could probably still stop me, Slip." And he sensed that she was awaiting his judgment, the last judgment any mere human would ever be allowed to levy upon her.

Slip shook his head and smiled at her, thinking of the slow-moving guardian angel that she would become. *Every race must arrive at this point in its history,* he suddenly realized. A few years or decades in which its future slavery or greatness rests on the goodwill of one or two persons. It could have been the Mailman. Thank God it was Ery instead.

And beyond those years or decades . . . for an instant,

Pollack came near to understanding things that had once been obvious. Processors kept getting faster, memories larger. What now took a planet's resources would someday be possessed by everyone. Including himself.

Beyond those years or decades . . . were millennia. And Ery.

—Vernor Vinge
San Diego
June 1979–January 1980

ALAN
URING

AFTERWORD
Marvin Minsky

In real life, you often have to deal with things you don't completely understand. You drive a car, not knowing how its engine works. You ride as passenger in someone else's car, not knowing how that driver works. And strangest of all, you sometimes drive yourself to work, not knowing how you work, yourself.

To me, the import of *True Names* is that it is about how we cope with things we don't understand. But, how do we ever understand anything in the first place? Almost always, I think, by using analogies in one way or another—to pretend that each alien thing we see resembles something we already know. When an object's internal workings are too strange, complicated, or unknown to deal with directly, we extract whatever parts of its behavior we can comprehend and represent them by familiar symbols—or the names of familiar things which we think do similar things. That way, we make each novelty at least appear to be like something which we know from the worlds of our own pasts. It is a great idea, that use of symbols; it lets our minds transform the strange into the commonplace. It is the same with names.

Right from the start, *True Names* shows us many forms of this idea, methods which use symbols, names, and images to make a novel world resemble one where we have been before. Remember the doors to Vinge's castle? Imagine that some architect has invented a new way to go from one place to another: a scheme that serves in some respects the normal functions of a door, but one whose form and mechanism is so entirely outside our past experience that, to see it, we'd never think of it as a door, nor guess what purposes to use it for. No matter: just superimpose, on its exterior, some decoration which reminds one of a door. We could clothe it in rectangular shape, or add to it a waist-high knob, or a push-plate with a sign lettered "EXIT" in red and white, or do whatever else may seem appropriate—and every visitor from Earth will know, without a conscious thought, that pseudo-portal's purpose, and how to make it do its job.

At first this may seem mere trickery; after all, this new invention, which we decorate to look like a door, is not really a door. It has none of what we normally expect a door to be, to wit: hinged, swinging slab of wood, cut into wall. The inner details are all wrong. Names and symbols, like analogies, are only partial truths; they work by taking many-levelled descriptions of different things and chopping off all of what seem, in the present context, to be their least essential details—that is, the ones which matter least to our intended purposes. But, still, what matters—when it comes to using such a thing—is that whatever symbol or icon, token or sign we choose should remind us of the use we seek—which, for that not-quite-door, should represent some way to go from one place to another. Who cares how it works, so long as it works! It does not even matter if that "door" leads to anywhere: in *True Names*, nothing ever leads anywhere; instead, the protagonists' bodies never move at all, but remain plugged-in to the network while programs change their representations of the simulated realities!

Ironically, in the world *True Names* describes, those representations actually do move from place to place—but only because the computer programs which do the work may be sent anywhere within the world-wide network of connections. Still, to the dwellers inside that network, all of this is inessential and imperceptible, since the physical locations of the computers themselves are normally not represented anywhere at all inside the worlds they simulate. It is only in the final acts of the novel, when those partially-simulated beings finally have to protect themselves against their entirely-simulated enemies, that the programs must keep track of where their mind-computers are; then they resort to using ordinary means, like military maps and geographic charts.

And strangely, this is also the case inside the ordinary brain: it, too, lacks any real sense of where it is. To be sure, most modern, educated people know that thoughts proceed inside the head—but that is something which no brain knows until it's told. In fact, without the help of education, a human brain has no idea that any such things as brains exist. Perhaps we tend to place the seat of thought behind the face, because that's where so many sense-organs are located. And even that impression is somewhat wrong: for example, the brain-centers for vision are far away from the eyes, away in the very back of the head, where no unaided brain would ever expect them to be.

In any case, the point is that the icons in *True Names* are not designed to represent the truth—that is, the truth of how the designated object, or program, works; that just is not an icon's job. An icon's purpose is, instead, to represent a way an object or a program can be used. And, since the idea of a use is in the user's mind—and not connected to the thing it represents—the form and figure of the icon must be suited to the symbols that the users have acquired in their own development. That is, it has to be connected to whatever mental processes are already one's most fluent, expressive, tools for expressing intentions. And that's why Roger represents his watcher the way his mind has learned to represent a frog.

This principle, of choosing symbols and icons which express the functions of entities—or rather, their users' intended attitudes toward them—was already second nature to the designers of earliest fast-interaction computer systems, namely, the early computer games which were, as Vernor Vinge says, the ancestors of the Other Plane in which the novel's main activities are set. In the 1970's the meaningful-icon idea was developed for personal computers by Alan Kay's research group at Xerox, but it was only in the early 1980's, after further work by Steven Jobs' research group at Apple Computer, that this concept entered the mainstream of the computer revolution, in the body of the Macintosh computer.

Over the same period, there have also been less-publicized attempts to develop iconic ways to represent, not what the programs do, but how they work. This would be of great value in the different enterprise of making it easier for programmers to make new programs from old ones. Such attempts have been less successful, on the whole, perhaps because one is forced to delve too far inside the lower-level details of how the programs work. But such difficulties are too transient to interfere with Vinge's vision, for there is evidence that he regards today's ways of programming—which use stiff, formal, inexpressive languages—as but an early stage of how great programs will be made in the future.

Surely the days of programming, as we know it, are numbered. We will not much longer construct large computer systems by using meticulous but conceptually impoverished procedural specifications. Instead, we'll express our intentions about what should be done, in terms, or gestures, or examples, at least as resourceful as our ordinary, everyday methods for expressing our wishes and convictions. Then these expressions will be submitted to immense, intelligent, intention-understanding programs which will themselves construct the actual, new programs. We shall no longer be burdened with the need to understand all the smaller details of how computer codes work. All of that will be left to those great utility programs, which will perform the arduous tasks of applying what we have embodied in them, once and for all, of what we know about the arts of lower-level programming. Then, once we learn better ways to tell computers what we want them to get done, we will be able to return to the more familiar realm of expressing our own wants and needs. *For, in the end, no user really cares about how a program works, but only about what it does—in the sense of the intelligible effects it has on other things with which the user is concerned.*

In order for that to happen, though, we will have to invent and learn to use new technologies for "expressing intentions". To do this, we will have to break away from our old, though still evolving, programming languages, which are useful only for describing processes. And this may be much harder than it sounds. For, it is easy enough to say that all we want to do is but to specify *what we want to happen*, using more familiar modes of expression. But this brings with it some very serious risks.

The first risk is that this exposes us to the consequences of self-deception. It is always tempting to say to oneself, when writing a program, or writing an essay, or, for that matter, doing almost anything, that *"I know what I would want, but I can't quite express it clearly enough"*. However, that concept itself reflects a too-simplistic self-image, which portrays one's own self as existing, somewhere in the heart of one's mind (so to speak), in the form of a pure, uncomplicated entity which has pure and unmixed wishes, intentions, and goals. This pre-Freudian image serves to excuse our frequent appearances of ambivalence; we convince ourselves that clarifying our intentions is a mere matter of straightening-out the input-output channels between our inner and outer selves. The trouble is, we simply aren't made that way, no matter how we may wish we were.

We incur another risk whenever we try to escape the responsibility of understanding how our wishes will be realized. It is always dangerous to leave much choice of means to any servants we may choose—no matter whether we program them or not. For, the larger the range of choice of methods they may use, to gain for us the ends we think we seek, the more we expose ourselves to possible accidents. We may not realize, perhaps until it is too late to turn back, that our goals were misinterpreted, perhaps even maliciously, as in such classic tales of fate as Faust, the Sorcerer's Apprentice, or The Monkey's Paw (by W.W. Jacobs).

The ultimate risk, though, comes when we greedy, lazy, master-minds are able at last to take that final step: to design goal-achieving programs which are programmed to make themselves grow increasingly powerful, by using learning and self-evolution methods which augment and enhance their own capabilities. It will be tempting to do this, not just for the gain in power, but just to decrease our own human effort in the consideration and formulation of our own desires. If some genie offered you three wishes, would not your first one be, *"Tell me, please, what is it that I want the most!"* The problem is that, with such powerful machines, it would require but the slightest accident of careless design for them to place their goals ahead of ours, perhaps the well-meaning purpose of protecting us from ourselves, as in *With Folded Hands*, by Jack Williamson),—or to protect us from an unsuspected enemy, as in *Colossus* by D.H. Jones, or because, like Arthur C. Clarke's HAL, the machine we have built considers us inadequate to the mission we ourselves have proposed, or, as in the case of Vernor Vinge's own Mailman, who teletypes its messages because it cannot spare the time to don disguises of dissimulated flesh, simply because the new machine has motives of its very own.

Now, what about the last and finally dangerous question which is asked toward *True Names'* end? Are those final scenes really possible, in which a human user starts to build itself a second, larger Self inside the machine? Is anything like that conceivable? And if it were, then would those simulated computer-people be in any sense the same as their human models before them; would they be genuine extensions of those real people? Or would they merely be new, artificial, person-things which resemble their originals only through some sort of structural coincidence? What if the aging Erythrina's simulation, unthinkably enhanced, is permitted to live on inside her new residence, more luxurious than Providence? What if we also suppose that she, once there, will be still inclined to share it with Roger—since no sequel should be devoid of romance—and that those two tremendous entities will love one another? Still, one must inquire, what would those super-beings share with those whom they were based upon? To answer that, we have to think more carefully about what those individuals were before. But, since these aren't real characters, but only figments of an author's mind, we'd better ask, instead, about the nature of our selves.

Now, once we start to ask about our selves, we'll have to ask how these, too, work—and this is what I see as the cream of the jest because, it seems to me, that inside every normal person's mind is, indeed, a certain portion, which we call the Self—but it, too, uses symbols and representations very much like the magic spells used by those players of the Inner World to work their wishes from their terminals. To explain this theory about the working of human consciousness, I'll have to compress some of the arguments from "The Society of Mind", my forthcoming book. In several ways, my image of what happens in the human mind resembles Vinge's image of how the players of the Other Plane have linked themselves into their networks of computing machines—by using superficial symbol-signs to control of host of systems which we do not fully understand.

Everybody knows that we humans understand far less about the insides of our minds, than what we know about the world outside. We know how ordinary objects work, but nothing of the great computers in our brains. Isn't it amazing we can think, not knowing what it means to think? Isn't it bizarre that we can get ideas, yet not be able to explain what ideas are. Isn't it strange how often we can better understand our friends than ourselves?

Consider again, how, when you drive, you guide the immense momentum of a car, not knowing how its engine works, or how its steering wheel directs the vehicle toward left or right. Yet, when one comes to think of it, don't we drive our bodies the same way? You simply set yourself to go in a certain direction and, so far as conscious thought is concerned, it's just like turning a mental steering wheel. All you are aware of is some general intention—*It's time to go: where is the door?*—and all the rest takes care of itself. But did you ever consider the complicated processes involved in such an ordinary act as, when you walk, changing the direction you're going in? It is not just a matter of, say, taking a larger or smaller step on one side, the way one changes course when rowing a boat. If that were all you did, when walking, you would tip over and fall toward the outside of the turn.

Try this experiment: watch yourself carefully while turning—and you'll notice that, before you start the turn, you tip yourself in advance; this makes you start to fall toward the inside of the turn; then, when you catch yourself on the next step, you end up moving in a different direction. When we examine that more closely, it all turns out to be dreadfully complicated: hundreds of interconnected muscles, bones, and joints are all controlled simultaneously, by interacting programs which locomotion-scientists still barely comprehend. Yet all your conscious mind need do, or say, or think, is *Go that way!*—assuming that it makes sense to speak of the conscious mind as thinking anything at all. So far as one can see, we guide the vast machines inside ourselves, not by using technical and insightful schemes based on knowing how the underlying mechanisms work, but by tokens, signs, and symbols which are entirely as fanciful as those of Vinge's sorcery. It even makes one wonder if it's fair for us to gain our ends by casting spells upon our helpless hordes of mental under-thralls.

Now, if we take this only one more step, we see that, just as we walk without thinking, we also think without thinking! That is, we just as casually exploit the agencies which carry out our mental work. Suppose you have a hard problem. You think about it for a while; then after a time you find a solution. Perhaps the answer comes to you suddenly; you get an idea and say, "Aha, I've got it. I'll do such and such." But then, were someone to ask how you did it, how you found the solution, you simply would not know how to reply. People usually are able to say only things like this:

"I suddenly realized . . ."
"I just got this idea . . ."
"It occurred to me that . . ."

If we really knew how our minds work, we wouldn't so often act on motives which we don't suspect, nor would we have such varied theories in psychology. Why, when we're asked how people come upon their good ideas, are we reduced to superficial reproductive metaphors, to talk about "conceiving" or "gestating", or even "giving birth" to thoughts? We even speak of "ruminating" or "digesting"—as though the mind were anywhere but in the head. If we could see inside our minds we'd surely say more useful things than "Wait. I'm thinking."

People frequently tell me that they're absolutely certain that no computer could ever be sentient, conscious, self-willed, or in any other way "aware" of itself. They're often shocked when I ask what makes them sure that they, themselves, possess these admirable qualities. The reply is that, if they're sure of anything at all, it is that *"I'm aware—hence I'm aware."*

Yet, what do such convictions really mean? Since "Self-awareness" ought to be an awareness of what's going on within one's mind, no realist could maintain for long that people really have much insight, in the literal sense of seeing in.

Isn't it remarkable how certainly we feel that we're self-aware—that we have such broad abilities to know what's happening inside ourselves? The evidence for that is weak, indeed. It is true that some people seem to have special excellences, which we sometimes call "insights", for assessing the attitudes and motivations for other people. And certain individuals even sometimes make good evaluations of themselves. But that doesn't justify our using names like insight or self-awareness for such abilities. Why not simply call them "person-sights" or "person-awareness?" Is there really reason to suppose that skills like these are very different from the ways we learn the other kinds of things we learn? Instead of seeing them as "seeing in," we could regard them as quite the opposite: just one more way of "figuring out." Perhaps we learn about ourselves the same ways that we learn about un-self-ish things.

The fact is, the parts of ourselves which we call "self aware" are only a small fraction of the entire mind. They work by building simulated worlds of their own—worlds which are greatly simplified, in comparison with either the real world outside, or with the immense computer systems inside the brain: systems which no one can pretend, today, to understand. And our worlds of simulated awareness are worlds of simple magic, wherein each and every imagined object is invested with meanings and purposes. Consider how one can but scarcely see a hammer except as something to hammer with, or see a ball except as something to throw and catch. Why are we so constrained to perceive things, not as they are, but as they can be used? *Because the highest levels of our minds are goal-directed problem-solvers.* That is to say that all the machines inside our heads evolved, originally, to meet various built-in or acquired needs, for comfort and nutrition, for defense and for reproduction. Later, over the past few million years, we evolved even more powerful sub-machines which, in ways we don't yet understand, seem to correlate and analyze to discover which kinds of actions cause which sorts of effects; in a word, to discover what we call knowledge. And though we often like to think that knowledge is abstract, and that our search for it is pure and good in itself—still, we ultimately use it for its ability to tell us what to do to gain whichever ends we seek (even when we conclude that in order to do that, we may first need to gain yet more and more knowledge). Thus, because, as we say, "knowledge is power", our knowledge itself is enmeshed in those webs of ways we reach our goals. And that's the key: it isn't any use for us to know, unless our knowledge tells us what to do. This is so wrought into the conscious mind's machinery that it seems too obvious to state: *no knowledge is of any use unless we have a use for it.*

Now we come to see the point of consciousness: it is the part of the mind most specialized for knowing how to use the other systems which lie hidden in the mind. But it is not a specialist in knowing how those systems actually work, inside themselves. Thus, as we said, one walks without much sense of how it's done. It's only when those systems start to fail to work well that consciousness becomes engaged with small details. That way, a person who has sustained an injured leg may start, for the first time, consciously to make theories about how walking works: *To turn to the left, I'll have to push myself that way*—and then one has to figure out, *with what*? It is often only when we're forced to face an unusually hard problem that we become more reflective, and try to understand more about how the rest of the mind ordinarily solves problems; at such times one finds oneself saying such things as, "Now I must get organized. Why can't I concentrate on the important questions and not get distracted by those other inessential details?"

It is mainly at such moments—the times when we get into trouble—that we come closer than usual to comprehending how our minds work, by engaging the little knowledge we have about those mechanisms, in order to alter or repair them. It is paradoxical that these are just the times when we say we are "confused", because it is very intelligent to know so much about oneself that one can say that—in contrast merely to being confused and not even knowing it. Still, we disparage and dislike awareness of confusion, not realizing what a high degree of self-representation it must involve. Perhaps that only means that consciousness is getting out of its depth, and isn't really suited to knowing that much about how things work. In any case, even our most "conscious" attempts at self-inspection still remain confined mainly to the pragmatic, magic world of symbol-signs, for no human being seems ever to have succeeded in using self-analysis to find out very much about the programs working underneath.

So this is the irony of *True Names*. Though Vinge tells the tale as though it were a science-fiction fantasy—it is in fact a realistic portrait of our own, real-life predicament! I say again that we work our minds in the same unknowing ways we drive our cars and our bodies, as the players of those futuristic games control and guide what happens in their great machines: by using symbols, spells and images—as well as secret, private names. The parts of us which we call "consciousness" sit, as it were, in front of cognitive computer-terminals, trying to steer and guide the great unknown engines of the mind, not by understanding how those mechanisms work, but simply by selecting names from menu-lists of symbols which appear, from time to time, upon our mental screen-displays.

But really, when one thinks of it, it scarcely could be otherwise! Consider what would happen if our minds indeed could really see inside themselves. What could possibly be worse than to be presented with a clear view of the trillion-wire networks of our nerve-cell connections? Our scientists have peered at fragments of those structures for years with powerful microscopes, yet failed to come up with comprehensive theories of what those networks do and how. How much more devastating it would be to have to see it all at once!

What about the claims of mystical thinkers that there are other, better ways to see the mind. One recommended way is learning how to train the conscious mind to stop its usual sorts of thoughts and then attempt (by holding very still) to see and hear the fine details of mental life. Would that be any different, or better, than seeing them through instruments? Perhaps—except that it doesn't face the fundamental problem of how to understand a complicated thing! For, if we suspend our usual ways of thinking, we'll be bereft of all the parts of mind already trained to interpret complicated phenomena. Anyway, even if one could observe and detect the signals which emerge from other, normally inaccessible portions of the mind, these probably would make no sense to the systems involved with consciousness, because they represent unusually low level details. To see why this is so, let's return once more to understanding such simple things as how we walk.

Suppose that, when you walk about, you were indeed able to see and hear the signals in your spinal cord and lower brain. Would you be able to make any sense of them? Perhaps, but not easily. Indeed, it is easy to do such experiments, using simple bio-feedback devices to make those signals audible and visible; the result is that one may indeed more quickly learn to perform a new skill, such as better using an injured limb. However, just as before, this does not appear to work through gaining a conscious understanding of how those circuits work; instead the experience is very much like business as usual; we gain control by acquiring just one more form of semi-conscious symbol-magic. Presumably, what happens is that a new control system is assembled somewhere in the nervous system, and interfaced with superficial signals we can know about. However, bio-feedback does not appear to provide any different insights into how learning works than do our ordinary, built-in senses.

In any case, our locomotion-scientists have been

tapping such signals for decades, using electronic instruments. Using those data, they have been able to develop various partial theories about the kinds of interactions and regulation-systems which are involved. However, these theories have not emerged from relaxed meditation about, or passive observation of those complicated biological signals; what little we have learned has come from deliberate and intense exploitation of the accumulated discoveries of three centuries of our scientists' and mathematicians' study of analytical mechanics and a century of newer theories about servo-control engineering. It is generally true in science that just observing things carefully rarely leads to new "insights" and understandings. One must first have at least the glimmerings of the form of a new theory, or of a novel way to describe: one needs a "new idea". For the "causes" and the "purposes" of what we observe are not themselves things that can be observed; to represent *them*, we need some other mental source to invent new magic tokens.

But where do we get the new ideas we need? For any single individual, of course, most concepts come from the societies and cultures that one grows up in. As for the rest of our ideas, the ones we "get" all by ourselves, these, too, come from societies—but, now, the ones inside our individual minds. For, a human mind is not in any real sense a single entity, nor does a brain have a single, central way to work. Brains do not secrete thought the way livers secrete bile; a brain consists of a huge assembly of sub-machines which each do different kinds of jobs—each useful to some other parts. For example, we use distinct sections of the brain for hearing the sounds of words, as opposed to recognizing other kinds of natural sounds or musical pitches. There is even solid evidence that there is a special part of the brain which is specialized for seeing and recognizing faces, as opposed to visual perception of other, ordinary things. I suspect that there are, inside the cranium, perhaps as many as a hundred kinds of computers, each with its own somewhat different architecture; these have been accumulating over the past four hundred million years of our evolution. They are wired together into a great multi-resource network of specialists, which each knows how to call on certain other specialists to get things done which serve its purposes. And each of these sub-brains uses its own styles of programming and its own forms of representations; there is no standard, universal language-code.

Accordingly, if one part of that Society of Mind were to inquire about another part, this probably would not work because they have such different languages and architectures. How could they understand one another, with so little in common? Communication is difficult enough between two different human tongues. But the signals used by the different portions of the human mind are even less likely to be even remotely as similar as two human dialects with sometimes-corresponding roots. More likely, they are simply too different to communicate at all—except through symbols which initiate their use.

Now, one might ask, *"Then, how do people doing different jobs communicate, when they have different backgrounds, thoughts, and purposes?"* The answer is that this problem is easier, because a person knows so much more than do the smaller fragments of that person's mind. And, besides, we all are raised in similar ways, and this provides a solid base of common knowledge. Even so, we overestimate how well we actually communicate. The many jobs that people do may seem different on the surface, but they are all very much the same, to the extent that they all have a common base in what we like to call "common sense"—that is, the knowledge shared by all of us. This means that we do not really need to tell each other as much as we suppose. Often, when we "explain" something, we scarcely explain anything new at all; instead, we merely show some examples of what we mean, and some non-examples; these indicate to the listener how to link up various structures already known. In short, we often just tell "which" instead of "how".

Consider how hard we find it to explain so many seemingly simple things. We can't say how to balance on a bicycle, or distinguish a picture from a real thing, or, even how to fetch a fact from memory. Again, one might complain, *It isn't fair to expect us to be able to put in words such things as seeing or balancing or remembering. Those are things we learned before we even learned to speak!* But, though that criticism is fair in some respects, it also illustrates how hard communication must be for all the subparts of the mind which never learned to talk at all—and these are most of what we are. The idea of "meaning" itself is really a matter of size and scale: it only makes sense to ask what something means in a system which is large enough to have many meanings. In very small systems, the idea of something having a meaning becomes as vacuous as saying that a brick is a very small house.

Now it is easy enough to say that the mind is a society, but that idea by itself is useless unless we can say more about how it is organized. If all those specialized parts were equally competitive, there would be only anarchy, and the more we learned, the less we'd be able to do. So there must be some kind of administration, perhaps organized roughly in hierarchies, like the divisions and subdivisions of an industry or of a human political society. What would those levels do? In all the large societies we know which work efficiently, the lower levels exercise the more specialized working skills, while the higher levels are concerned with longer-range plans and goals. And this is another fundamental reason why it is so hard to translate between our conscious and unconscious thoughts! The kinds of terms and symbols we use on the conscious level are primarily for expressing our goals and plans for using what we believe we can do—while the workings of those lower level resources are represented in unknown languages of process and mechanism. So when our conscious probes try to descend into the myriads of smaller and smaller sub-machines which make the mind, they encounter alien representations, used for increasingly specialized purposes.

The trouble is, these tiny inner "languages" soon become incomprehensible, for a reason which is simple and inescapable. This is not the same as the familiar difficulty of translating between two different human languages; we understand the nature of *that* problem: it is that human languages are so huge and rich that it is hard to narrow meanings down: we call that "ambiguity". But, when we try to understand the tiny languages at the lowest levels of the mind, we have the opposite problem—because *the smaller be two languages, the harder it will be to translate between them, not because there are too many meanings but too few. The fewer things two systems do, the less likely that something one of them can do will correspond to anything at all the other one can do.* And then, no translation is possible. Why is this worse than when there is much ambiguity? Because, although that problem seems very hard, still, even when a problem seems hopelessly complicated, there always can be hope. But, when a problem is hopelessly simple, there can't be any hope at all!

Now, finally, let's return to the question of how much a simulated life inside a world inside a machine could be like our ordinary, real life, "out here"? My answer, as you know by now, is that it could be very much the same—since we, ourselves, as we've seen, already exist as processes imprisoned in machines inside machines. Our mental worlds are already filled with wondrous, magical, symbol-signs, which add to everything we "see" a meaning and significance.

All educated people already know how different is our mental world from the "real world" our scientists know. For, consider the table in your dining room; your conscious mind sees it as having a familiar function, form, and purpose: a table is "a thing to put things on". However, our science tells us that this is only in the mind; all that's "really there" is a society of countless molecules; the table seems to hold its shape, only because some of those molecules are constrained to vibrate near one another, because of certain properties of the force-fields which keep them from pursuing independent paths. Similarly, when you hear a spoken word, your mind attributes sense and meaning to that sound—whereas, in physics, the word is merely a fluctuating pressure on your ear, caused by the collisions of myriads of molecules of air—that is, of particles whose distances, this time are less constrained.

And so—let's face it now, once and for all: each one of us already has experienced what it is like to be simulated by a computer!

"Ridiculous," most people say, at first: "I certainly don't feel like a machine!"

But what makes us so sure of that? How could one claim to know how something feels, until one has experienced it? Consider that either you are a machine or you're not. Then, if, as you say, you aren't a machine, you are scarcely in any position of authority to say how it feels to be a machine.

"Very well, but, surely then, if I were a machine, then at least I would be in a position to know that!"

No. That is only an innocently grandiose presumption, which amounts to claiming that, "I think, therefore I know how thinking works." But as we've seen, there are so many levels of machinery between our conscious thoughts and how they're made that saying such a thing is as absurd as to say, "I drive, therefore I know how engines work!"

"Still, even if the brain is a kind of computer, you must admit that its scale is unimaginably large. A human brain contains many billions of brain cells—

and, probably, each cell is extremely complicated by itself. Then, each cell is interlinked in complicated ways to thousands or millions of other cells. You can use the word "machine" for that but, surely, no one could ever build anything of that magnitude!"

I am entirely sympathetic with the spirit of this objection. When one is compared to a machine, one feels belittled, as though one is being regarded as trivial. And, indeed, such a comparison in truly insulting—so long as the name "machine" still carries the same meaning it had in times gone by. For thousands of years, we have used such words to arouse images of pulleys, levers, locomotives, typewriters, and other simple sorts of things; similarly, in modern times, the word "computer" has evoked thoughts about adding and subtracting digits, and storing them unchanged in tiny so-called "memories". However those words no longer serve our new purposes, to describe machines that think like us; for such uses, those old terms have become false names for what we want to say. Just as "house" may stand for either more, or nothing more, than wood and stone, our minds may be described as nothing more, and, yet far more, then just machines.

As to the question of scale itself, those objections are almost wholly out-of-date. They made sense in 1950, before any computer could store even a mere million bits. They still made sense in 1960, when a million bits costs a million dollars. But, today, that same amount of money costs but a hundred dollars (and our governments have even made the dollars smaller, too)—and there already exist computers with billions of bits.

The only thing missing is most of the knowledge we'll need to make such machines intelligent. Indeed, as you might guess from all this, the focus of research in Artificial Intelligence should be to find good ways, as Vinge's fantasy suggests, to connect structures with functions through the use of symbols. When, if ever, will that get done? Never say "Never".

VERNOR VINGE

A Hugo and Nebula Award finalist for *True Names*, he is also the author of *The Peace War, Grimm's World*, and a number of short stories. A mathematician and computer scientist, he has published articles in magazines such as *Omni*. He teaches at San Diego State University.

BOB WALTERS

His illustrations have graced the pages of SF magazines such as *Analog* and *Isaac Asimov's SF Magazine*. He has also done a great deal of scientific illustration for college texts, as well as general advertising illustration. He lives in Philadelphia, Pennsylvania.

MARVIN MINSKY

Considered by many to be the father of Artificial Intelligence, he has written especially for this book an essay on the nature of intelligence, natural and artificial. He is the director of the Artificial Intelligence laboratory at the Massachusetts Institute of Technology.